LIVING IN THE SUITCASE

DEEPAK SHARMA

Contents

Contents

"A suitcase holds more than clothes; it holds aspirations, sacrifices, and untold stories. This isn't about the journey—it's about the weight we choose to carry.
- Deepak Sharma"

SYNOPSIS

In Living in the Suitcase, Deepak Sharma presents a compelling narrative that captures the relentless pace of modern professional life and its emotional undercurrents. The story follows Vikram, a seasoned professional whose life revolves around boardrooms, red-eye flights, and fleeting family moments. On the surface, he's a picture of success, but beneath lies a man grappling with the deeper questions of purpose, happiness, and the toll of his relentless pursuit.

Through the eyes of Vikram, readers journey into the realities of a life spent on the move—missed milestones, silent sacrifices, and the duality of living for both recognition and inner contentment. Alongside him, a cast of characters brings depth and texture to the narrative, reflecting the collective experience of families, colleagues, and friends impacted by his choices.

At its heart, the book delves into the obsession with societal ideals—why parents dream of their children as engineers or doctors, why professionals strive for titles over contentment, and why breaking these cycles feels so daunting. Yet, it also offers hope, highlighting the power of introspection, small wins, and new perspectives to rewrite one's story.

Living in the Suitcase is more than a tale of struggle—it's a reflective journey that resonates deeply with those caught between ambition and meaning.

A blend of personal growth, societal critique, and emotional exploration, this novel challenges readers to confront their own 'suitcases' and unpack what truly matters.

PREFACE

A suitcase is more than a carrier of clothes and essentials—it's a metaphor for the lives we live. For some, it's a symbol of ambition, always packed for the next destination. For others, it's a weight of sacrifices, memories, and dreams that never found a home.

This book isn't just about the physical journey of living in a suitcase. It's about the emotional and psychological spaces we inhabit while we chase goals, fulfil obligations, and navigate expectations. It's about the spaces we leave behind—family, roots, and a sense of self—and the new ones we try to build amidst the chaos.

As I set out to write this book, I didn't imagine how much it would mirror the lives of many. From the professional constantly on the move to the young dreamer chasing freedom, and even the silent observer balancing choices, this story speaks to everyone who has ever felt torn between where they are and where they want to be.

You'll meet Vikram here, but in his story, you may recognize your own. You'll see the layers—the pride of accomplishment, the guilt of absence, the silent battles fought within, and the obsession to 'get it right.'

"Living in the Suitcase" is not about finding an answer. It's about reflecting on the journey.

It's about the choices we make, the lives we touch, and the moments that make us pause and ask—what's it all for?

Welcome to the journey. Let's unpack it, one chapter at a time.

With gratitude
Deepak Sharma

Acknowledgements

Every journey is a story woven from countless threads—of love, sacrifices, guidance, and shared moments. "Living in the Suitcase" is no different. It carries the essence of everyone who has walked alongside me, supported me, and shaped the reflections within these pages.

To my parents: Your quiet resilience and unyielding belief in the power of effort have been my compass through life. You taught me the value of standing tall, even when the weight of expectations loomed heavy. This book, in many ways, echoes the lessons you've imparted.

To my wife: Your strength, understanding, and unwavering support have been my constant, even when life's journeys kept us apart. You are the heartbeat of my story, grounding me while I wandered the paths of discovery. To our children, who see the world through eyes unclouded by expectations—your laughter reminds me why we strive to break cycles, to build futures not bound by tradition but inspired by possibility.

To my mentors and colleagues: Your shared wisdom and camaraderie have deeply influenced the pages of this book. The lessons learned in meeting rooms, on the road, and during those long conversations over chai have found their place here.

To the countless professionals who live their lives on the go: This book is a tribute to you. It seeks to echo your silent struggles, fleeting victories, and the endless chase for something greater. Your stories are the threads that bind this narrative together.

Finally, to my readers: This journey is now yours. The story of Vikram may reflect pieces of your own life—its highs and lows, its questions and revelations. My hope is that it stirs reflection and sparks conversations you've been waiting to have, with yourself or those around you.

This book began with scattered thoughts, hurried notes scribbled during airport layovers, and conversations that stayed with me long after they ended. It has become more than just words; it's a mirror to a world many of us live but seldom pause to truly see.

Thank you for joining me on this journey.

With heartfelt gratitude,
Deepak Sharma

DISCLAIMER

This book is a work of narrative non-fiction. While it draws inspiration from real-life experiences, observations, and interactions, the characters, incidents, and dialogues are products of the author's imagination or used in a fictionalized manner. Any resemblance to actual persons, living or dead, or events is purely coincidental.

The book is intended to provoke thought, encourage reflection, and share perspectives on professional and personal journeys. It does not intend to critique or challenge any specific profession, belief system, or societal norm. Instead, it seeks to explore universal themes of ambition, purpose, and the intricate balance between personal and professional commitments.

The views and opinions expressed are those of the author and should not be taken as professional advice. Readers are encouraged to interpret the narrative within their own context and experiences.

Above all, this book is a celebration of the human spirit—its struggles, growth, and capacity for change.

Deepak Sharma

I

The Weigh of a Suitcase

The taxi pulled up to yet another airport, its engine sputtering to a stop under the fluorescent lights of the terminal. Vikram didn't flinch; he'd been here so many times, at so many airports, he could do this blindfolded. He glanced at his watch—another flight, another city, another meeting.

The driver handed him the receipt without saying a word. Vikram paid in silence, his mind already somewhere else. He grabbed his suitcase, a well-worn, reliable companion, and made his way to the security line.

As he stood there, waiting, he couldn't help but notice the families around him. Parents walking with children, suitcases filled with toys, snacks, and all the things that made family travel a different experience. He had his own suitcase, sure, but this one was always packed with expectations—his father's hopes, his mother's dreams, his own sense of duty.

He thought about his last call with his mom. "How are you, beta?

Any good news?" The words were sweet, but they carried the weight of everything he hadn't told her. He couldn't bring himself to say the truth: that despite the promotions, the sales figures, the recognition—he still felt like he was running, chasing something that wasn't even clear anymore.

The gates were announced, and Vikram joined the line, as automatic as the years of travel behind him. The noise of the terminal faded into the background as his mind wandered. The same questions kept popping up, uninvited.

Is this what success is? Is this all there is?

The gates opened, and Vikram walked down the jet bridge, the hum of the plane's engines a constant reminder of how far he'd come from where he started. But there was no satisfaction in the thought, just a quiet knowing that the next flight would be the same.

He sat in his seat, staring out the window as the plane taxied. For a moment, the blur of the airport below seemed to offer him a sense of clarity. He wasn't running from something—he was running toward something. But what?

As the plane ascended, leaving the city below him, Vikram felt the weight of his suitcase settle on his lap. He leaned back in his seat, eyes closed for a moment. Somewhere, in that vast sky, he was supposed to find the answers.

But for now, he would just fly.

II

The Hidden Cost of Success

Vikram had grown used to the sound of the city fading away as the plane took off. Each ascent, each lift off the ground, felt like a personal departure—leaving something behind, even though he wasn't sure what it was anymore. The same sensation washed over him every time: the feeling of moving away from what was familiar, yet never quite reaching where he was supposed to be.

The flight was long, the hours slipping by in that strange timelessness that came with air travel. He sat in his seat, the seatbelt fastened, his eyes half-closed as the rhythmic hum of the engines lulled him into a quiet state. There was a strange calmness that came with being in the air. Up here, nothing could reach him. There was no deadline, no client call, no presentation to prepare for. Just him and the space above the clouds.

But even here, there was a familiar weight pressing down on him—the weight of his thoughts, the weight of his decisions.

As the plane began its descent, he opened his eyes, glancing out the window at the sprawling city below. Lights flickered in the distance, buildings casting long shadows on the streets. Another city, another chapter in the journey. He had become used to the pattern of it all—the flights, the cities, the brief encounters with people whose names he would forget by the time he left. But it was more than just the cities. It was the constant feeling that there was something more, something just beyond his grasp.

He thought back to the message from his mother earlier that morning. "Beta, when will you be home? You've been traveling so much. We miss you." The words were soft, filled with love, but they carried an unspoken message that Vikram couldn't ignore.

Home. It was a word that didn't quite belong to him anymore, not in the way it used to. When he was younger, home had been the place where he felt anchored. It was where he could rest, recharge, and be himself. But now, it felt like home was the place he ran away from, a place filled with expectations that were too heavy for him to carry.

He could almost hear his father's voice in his head: "You must work hard, beta. Do not waste time. Achieve what I could not. I have given you everything, now you must repay that with success."

Vikram leaned back in his seat, the words echoing in his mind. His father had worked tirelessly, sacrificing everything for a future that was supposed to be better than his own. Vikram had been the one to inherit that dream, the one to carry it forward. But what if that dream wasn't his own? What if the life he was living wasn't the one he had imagined for himself?

The cabin lights dimmed, and the flight attendants began their descent preparations, but Vikram barely noticed. His thoughts had taken him elsewhere. He wondered if anyone ever felt like this—lost in the middle of their success, unsure of what they were working towards anymore.

As the plane touched down, Vikram's phone buzzed with a message from Sameer, his colleague, a constant reminder of the world that awaited him outside the window.

"Vikram, I need your inputs on the new proposal. We're meeting the client tomorrow at 10 AM. Don't forget to prep."

Vikram sighed, rubbing his temples. Sameer was a good guy, a reliable colleague, but there was always something about the work that gnawed at him. It was a constant cycle of meetings, proposals, presentations—always working towards the next goal, but never really reaching it. The pressure to perform was never-ending.

But what did that even mean? What was the point of all this? To sell more? To be recognized? To climb higher and higher, always on the move, never stopping to catch his breath?

The thought of his mother's message resurfaced, and Vikram felt a pang in his chest. We miss you. His family had always wanted the best for him. They had sacrificed so much for him to have this life—this fast-paced, high-stakes existence. But Vikram wasn't sure if they understood what it had cost him. The nights on the road, the constant strain of trying to meet expectations, the feeling of never being able to catch up.

He stepped off the plane and into the terminal, the familiar buzz of airport noise surrounding him. The rush of people, the flurry of activity—it was all so normal now. The taxi ride to the hotel felt like a blur, and before he knew it, he was in the hotel room again, suitcase by the door.

He stood in front of the mirror for a moment, staring at his reflection. The man in the mirror seemed like a stranger—someone who had been moulded by the expectations of others, someone who had lost touch with who he truly was.

Vikram hadn't chosen this life, not really. It had been laid out for him, piece by piece, starting with his father's dream. It was a dream of success, of accomplishment, of proving that the sacrifices had been worth it. But as the years went by, Vikram had begun to wonder if there was more to life than just achievement.

He walked over to the desk and opened his journal, the pen in his hand feeling foreign after so long. He hadn't written in it for months, and now, the words seemed to come slower than usual.

"What do I really want?"

The question hung in the air, as heavy and elusive as ever. Vikram scribbled it down, then stared at it for a long moment. He didn't know the answer. Not yet. But maybe that was okay. Maybe he didn't have to have it all figured out.

He closed the journal, took a deep breath, and walked over to the window. The city outside was just as chaotic as the last one, just as full of possibility, and just as empty. He wondered if it would ever stop feeling like this—a constant search, a constant longing for something that always seemed just out of reach.

In the silence of his room, Vikram realized that the greatest cost of success wasn't in the hours he spent working, the cities he travelled to, or the deals he closed. It was in the quiet moments, the ones that came when he was alone with his thoughts, when he realized that the life he had built for himself wasn't truly his own.

And for the first time in a long time, Vikram didn't know what the next step was. But maybe that was okay too. Maybe it was time to stop chasing, to stop running, and to just be.

III

The Long Walk Home

The streets of the city were alive with their usual chaos—auto-rickshaws honking, street vendors shouting over each other, and pedestrians weaving through the traffic with an ease that came from years of practice. Vikram stepped out of the office building, his laptop bag slung over one shoulder and the weight of the day pressing down on him. It was late, and the roads shimmered with the glow of streetlights reflected on wet asphalt.

He could've called for a cab. It would've been the practical thing to do, but practicality wasn't what he needed tonight. Instead, he began to walk.

The city had a way of swallowing you whole if you let it. Its energy was infectious but also exhausting. For every moment of triumph, there were a hundred moments of doubt, of second-guessing, of wondering if it was all worth it. Tonight, Vikram wasn't in the mood for the noise of the city or the buzz of his phone. He needed the quiet that came with walking.

The streets became less crowded as he moved away from the commercial district, the office towers giving way to smaller shops and residential buildings. He passed a chai stall, its steam curling into the night air, and paused. The vendor, an older man with tired eyes but a warm smile, handed him a glass of tea.

"Long day, bhaiya?" the man asked, his voice kind.

Vikram nodded, taking a sip. The chai was sweet, the kind of sweetness that felt indulgent, almost like a reminder that small pleasures still existed in the world. He stood there for a moment, watching the city around him. A group of college students laughed as they huddled around another stall, their carefree energy a stark contrast to the weight he carried.

As he finished the tea, Vikram handed the glass back to the vendor and thanked him. The man nodded in return, a silent exchange of understanding between two strangers.

The walk continued, and with each step, Vikram felt a little lighter. The noise of his thoughts, always so loud, began to quiet down. He found himself thinking about his family, about the life he had left behind when he moved to the city.

His mother used to wait up for him whenever he came home late, even during his college days. She'd pretend to be asleep on the sofa, but Vikram always knew better. She'd make him sit down, heat up the dinner she'd kept aside, and listen as he talked about his day.

He smiled at the memory, but it was bittersweet. How long had it been since he'd had a proper conversation with her? These days, their calls were brief, filled with updates and reassurances. She never complained, but he could hear the unspoken worry in her voice.

As he turned a corner, Vikram's thoughts shifted to his father. The man was a paradox—proud yet humble, stern yet caring. He had spent his entire life working in a small-town government office, saving every rupee to ensure Vikram and his sister had opportunities he never did.

"Beta, I only want you to have a better life than mine." His father's words echoed in his mind.

Vikram had taken those words to heart, using them as fuel during his college years, during his first job, and every moment since. But now, he wondered if he had misunderstood what his father meant. Was this what a "better life" looked like? A life lived out of a suitcase, constantly on the move, chasing goals that never felt fulfilling?

The sound of his phone buzzing snapped him out of his thoughts. It was Sameer again, this time with a voice note.

"Vikram, just a quick reminder about tomorrow's meeting. I need your thoughts on the client pitch before noon. Let me know when you're free to discuss."

He sighed, slipping the phone back into his pocket. The night, which had felt almost serene a moment ago, seemed heavier now. The walk, his attempt to find some clarity, had only brought more questions.

But then, as he neared his apartment building, something caught his eye. A small girl, no older than seven or eight, was sitting on the steps of a closed shop, her head resting on her knees. Beside her was a woman, likely her mother, trying to calm a crying toddler.

The scene was ordinary, the kind of thing Vikram would've overlooked on any other day. But tonight, it struck a chord.

The girl looked up, her eyes meeting his for a brief moment. There was no anger, no sadness—just a quiet resilience that Vikram couldn't quite place. She turned away as her mother handed her a piece of bread, a small dinner for a family that clearly had little to spare.

Vikram hesitated. He wanted to help, to do something, but he wasn't sure what. Instead, he walked on, the image of the family lingering in his mind.

By the time he reached his apartment, the city was quiet. He unlocked the door, stepping into the stillness of his home. The suitcase sat by the corner, its presence a constant reminder of the life he led.

He set his bag down and walked to the balcony, staring out at the city below. The lights twinkled, the streets hummed with distant activity, and somewhere out there, the family he'd passed was likely settling in for the night.

Vikram's thoughts turned to his own family. He wondered what his parents would think if they knew how he felt—if they understood that, despite everything, he still felt like he was searching for something.

As the night deepened, Vikram made a silent promise to himself. He didn't know what he was searching for, but he knew he couldn't keep running in circles. The journey had to mean something.

For now, though, he closed his eyes and let the city's rhythm carry him to sleep.

IV
Crossroads at Dawn

The dawn light seeped through the cracks in the curtains, casting soft, golden streaks across Vikram's apartment. The alarm clock buzzed faintly, but he was already awake, sitting by the window with a cup of black coffee. The city was stirring, its early-morning sounds carrying a strange kind of calm—the distant hum of buses, the chirping of birds, the faint chatter of street vendors setting up shop.

He had hardly slept, his mind restless with memories and questions. The image of the young girl and her family from the night before lingered like a shadow, mingling with the echoes of his parents' voices from years past.

The world had always been clear in its expectations. Do well in school. Get into a good college. Land a stable job. Provide for your family. Secure your future. And yet, here he was—on paper, successful, but carrying a hollow sense of something unfinished.

His phone lit up on the desk. A message from Sameer:

"Don't forget to review the pitch deck. Clients are tough, but we can nail this."

Vikram stared at the message for a moment before putting the phone on silent. He'd deal with it later.

Sameer: The Silent Coach

The day unfolded as expected—meetings, presentations, and deadlines blurring into each other. Sameer, his manager, was his usual self—sharp, efficient, and seemingly unbothered by the chaos.

"You've got to be concise, Vikram. We're dealing with a new audience here," Sameer said, leaning over Vikram's laptop as they reviewed the client presentation.

Vikram nodded, making notes as Sameer continued. But his mind kept wandering to their conversation from months ago. Sameer wasn't just a manager; he was a silent coach, a mirror who had once asked Vikram a question that still lingered.

"What do you really want out of this job?"

Vikram had laughed it off at the time, offering some rehearsed response about career growth and financial security. But the question had stuck with him, resurfacing in quiet moments like this one.

Later that evening, Vikram found himself at the same chai stall from the night before. The vendor smiled as if expecting him.

"Back again, bhaiya?" the man asked, pouring the tea.

Vikram nodded, taking the glass. He looked around, noticing the same group of college students laughing and talking animatedly. They were so full of energy, so unburdened by the weight of expectations.

"Do you have kids?" Vikram asked suddenly, surprising even himself.

The vendor chuckled. "Yes, two. Both are studying. My son wants to be an engineer, and my daughter... she wants to teach."

"Engineer, huh?" Vikram said, smiling faintly.

"Yes. It's not easy, but we do what we can. Education is everything, no? A better life starts there," the man said, his tone both hopeful and determined.

Vikram nodded, taking another sip of chai. The man's words echoed his father's, and for a moment, he saw a reflection of his own family in the vendor's simple dream.

The Unseen Struggles

As Vikram walked home, his thoughts circled back to the obsession that seemed to drive so many families—the relentless pursuit of security, respect, and recognition. His parents had made sacrifices he could never repay, driven by the same hope the chai vendor had for his children.

It wasn't about becoming an engineer or a doctor or anything else, really. It was about ensuring that the next generation had choices, opportunities that weren't dictated by necessity but by aspiration.

But somewhere along the way, Vikram wondered, had the obsession turned into a cage? For every child who thrived under the pressure, how many stumbled? For every "better life" achieved, how many dreams were quietly extinguished?

A New Resolve

Back at his apartment, Vikram sat down at his desk. He opened his laptop, not to work on the pitch deck but to jot down his thoughts. He wasn't much of a writer, but tonight, he needed to make sense of the jumble in his mind.

He wrote about the chai vendor, about his father's words, about the little girl on the steps. He wrote about the unspoken fears and the quiet resilience he saw in the people around him.

By the time he finished, the sun had set, and the city was alive again with its nightly chaos. Vikram closed the laptop, feeling a strange mix of exhaustion and clarity.

For the first time in a long while, he felt like he was beginning to understand what he was searching for.

V

The Turning Point

The conference room was unusually quiet, a stark contrast to the usual buzz of office chatter. Vikram stood at the head of the table, clicking through slides with a practiced ease. The client, a middle-aged man with a calculating gaze, nodded occasionally but offered no feedback.

Vikram could feel the weight of the room pressing down on him. This wasn't just a presentation; it was a test.

"And this brings us to our proposed solution," Vikram concluded, stepping back slightly, his voice steady despite the knot in his stomach.

The client exchanged a glance with his team. There was a pause—a silence so heavy it felt like it could crush him.

Finally, the man spoke. "Interesting approach. Let me think about it and get back to you."

It was the polite corporate equivalent of a shrug, and Vikram knew it.

A Familiar Pattern

Back at his desk, Vikram replayed the meeting in his mind, dissecting every word and gesture. It wasn't the first time he'd faced this kind of lukewarm response, and it wouldn't be the last.

He glanced at the corner of his desk where a framed photo of his family sat—a reminder of why he was here, why he pushed himself through moments like this.

His phone buzzed. A message from his mother.

"Did you eat? Don't skip meals."

Vikram smiled faintly, typing back a quick reply before leaning back in his chair.

The Waiting Family

Dinner that night was a solitary affair—instant noodles and a leftover paratha from lunch. As he ate, his thoughts drifted to his parents. They were waiting for him to visit, as they always were, asking the same questions every time they spoke:

"When will you come home? Are you eating well? Are you saving money?"

Their questions were simple, but Vikram knew they carried layers of worry and hope. They had given up so much to ensure he had the life they had dreamed of, and he often wondered if he was living up to those dreams.

He thought of his father's tired hands, his mother's quiet prayers, and the countless sacrifices they had made—sacrifices that had shaped the man he was today.

A Late-Night Walk

Unable to shake the restlessness, Vikram decided to go for a walk. The city was alive with its usual chaos—horns blaring, street vendors calling out, couples strolling hand in hand.

He found himself wandering aimlessly, his feet carrying him to the park near his apartment. It was quieter here, the noise of the city fading into the background.

Vikram sat on a bench, watching as a group of teenagers played cricket under the dim glow of a streetlamp. Their laughter echoed through the night, unburdened and carefree.

For a moment, he envied them.

An Unfinished Dream

As he sat there, a memory surfaced—one he hadn't thought about in years.

He was twelve, standing in the corner of the living room while his father spoke to a guest. The man had come to discuss an investment opportunity, but what Vikram remembered most was his father's voice—hopeful, determined, but tinged with uncertainty.

"This could be the break we need," his father had said, glancing at Vikram as if to say, *I'm doing this for you.*

The deal had fallen through, and Vikram had seen his father's disappointment, though he never spoke of it. That memory had stayed with him, a silent reminder of the dreams his father had deferred so that Vikram could chase his own.

Back at his apartment, Vikram opened his journal—a habit he had picked up in college but abandoned in recent years.

He hesitated for a moment before writing:

What does success really mean? Is it the recognition, the money, the stability? Or is it something more—a feeling, a purpose, a legacy?

The words felt incomplete, but they were a start.

As he closed the journal, Vikram felt a flicker of something he hadn't felt in a long time—clarity, or perhaps the beginning of it.

VI
Crossroads at Midnight

The hum of the office grew softer as the clock approached midnight. Most of Vikram's colleagues had long left, but he sat alone at his desk, bathed in the blue glow of his laptop. The pitch deck he had been fine-tuning for hours seemed no closer to perfection. His hand hovered over the delete key, tempted to start over for the fourth time.

A small stack of sticky notes lay next to his keyboard—reminders of edits suggested by his manager, half of which felt like conflicting instructions. The presentation wasn't due until Monday morning, but the pressure to excel—to make this pitch flawless—gnawed at him.

As he leaned back, stretching his cramped fingers, Vikram's eyes wandered to his journal lying beside him. A pen tucked neatly into its spine, the notebook beckoned him like an old friend.

He flipped it open to a blank page, the paper catching the faint breeze of the office air conditioning. After a brief hesitation, he wrote:

"Why does this matter so much?"

He paused, staring at the words. The question hung in the air, heavier than the silence around him. It wasn't the pitch that mattered. It was something deeper—a need for recognition, for proof that he was on the right path, for a sign that all the sacrifices were worth it.

His pen hovered again, and this time, the words flowed freely:

"What if I fail? What if I never get there? And... where exactly is 'there'?"

The sound of the janitor's mop sloshing down the hallway jolted him out of his thoughts. Closing the journal, he slid it back into his bag and reached for his phone. It was time to go home.

The streets outside were deserted, the city's chaos replaced by an eerie stillness. Vikram walked toward the corner where a lone tea stall remained open, its warm light spilling onto the pavement.

The chaiwala, a wiry man in his forties, greeted him with a smile. "Late night again, saab?"

Vikram nodded, handing over a few coins. As he sipped the steaming tea, the aroma and warmth reminded him of simpler times—nights spent at home with his parents, his mother insisting on making chai no matter how late he worked.

He thought about his father, who had once said, "Beta, stability is the real success. Find a good job, work hard, and you'll be happy." At the time, it had sounded so simple, so achievable. Now, standing under the harsh fluorescent bulb of a roadside stall, Vikram wondered if stability was even possible in a world that demanded constant hustle.

"Saab," the chaiwala interrupted his thoughts, "you work so late. Big job, hai na?"

Vikram smiled faintly. "Big job, yes. Big life? Not sure."

The chaiwala chuckled. "Life is what you make of it. My son studies in college now—first in our family. That's why I work late too. Dreams cost money."

Dreams cost money. The words lingered in Vikram's mind as he walked back to his car. Dreams didn't just cost money—they cost time, relationships, and sometimes, pieces of oneself.

The next morning, Vikram found himself in a bustling train station, heading to his hometown for the weekend. The platform was alive with activity—hawkers selling samosas and newspapers, children tugging at their parents' hands, and the unmistakable sound of announcements blaring over the intercom.

As he boarded the train, Vikram thought about the chaiwala's son. He thought about his own parents, who had invested everything into his education, pushing him to achieve what they couldn't. Wasn't that the story of every middle-class family? A relentless cycle of sacrifices and expectations, each generation trying to give the next a better start.

Settling into his seat, Vikram watched the landscape blur past the window. He felt a pang of guilt—he hadn't visited home in months. His parents rarely complained, but their quiet acceptance made it worse.

The train rocked gently as it sped through the countryside, and Vikram's thoughts drifted to the presentation waiting for him on Monday. It was ironic, he realized, how much of his life revolved around convincing others—clients, colleagues, even himself—that he was on the right track.

For a brief moment, he allowed himself to wonder: *What if I wasn't?*

As the train pulled into his hometown station, Vikram spotted his father waiting on the platform. His hair had grown greyer since Vikram's last visit, and his once-straight posture was slightly hunched. Yet his face lit up with a smile as soon as he saw his son.

"Beta!" his father called out, waving enthusiastically. Vikram waved back, his chest tightening with a mix of joy and guilt.

The drive home was quiet, punctuated only by his father's occasional questions about work. Vikram answered in monosyllables, avoiding details. It wasn't that he didn't want to share—it was just that he didn't know how to explain the gnawing uncertainty that had taken root in his mind.

As they entered the house, the smell of freshly made parathas greeted them. His mother appeared from the kitchen, wiping her hands on her saree. "You've lost weight," she said, frowning. "You work too hard."

Vikram laughed it off, but her words stayed with him. That night, as he lay in his childhood bed, staring at the ceiling fan, he thought about what his parents had given up to get him here.

Stability, comfort, dreams—they had sacrificed it all so that he could chase his own.

And now, here he was, still chasing

VII
Conversations in the Quiet

The smell of incense filled the air, blending with the faint aroma of parathas from the kitchen. Morning light streamed through the sheer curtains of Vikram's childhood bedroom, highlighting the faded posters on the wall. A cricket legend stared down from one, his confident smile a reminder of simpler times when Vikram's dreams had revolved around hitting sixes, not meeting targets.

He sat cross-legged on the bed, flipping through his journal. Pages filled with hurried thoughts and occasional doodles stared back at him. A recurring question caught his eye: *What's the endgame?*

Before he could dwell on it, his mother's voice called out, "Breakfast is ready!"

In the dining room, his parents were already seated. His father was reading the newspaper, glasses perched on his nose, while his mother fussed over a plate of buttered parathas.

"Beta, you barely eat in the city. Look at you—so thin," she said, piling more food onto his plate.

Vikram smiled. "Ma, I'm fine. If I eat any more, I'll fall asleep before lunch."

His father folded the newspaper and looked at him. "So, how's work?"

The question was simple, but the weight of it pressed down on Vikram. He hesitated before replying, "It's… busy. Lots of projects."

His father nodded, his expression unreadable. "Busy is good. It means you're doing well."

Vikram wanted to argue, to explain that busyness didn't always mean progress, but he stopped himself. Instead, he asked, "How's the shop?"

A spark lit up in his father's eyes. "Good. Your uncle and I are thinking of expanding—maybe adding a few more items to the inventory. People trust us, you know. They know we'll only sell quality goods."

There it was again: *trust.* It was the cornerstone of his father's life and work, a quiet pride in doing things the right way. Vikram couldn't help but wonder if he had inherited that same drive, or if his pursuit of success had led him down a different path entirely.

Later that day, Vikram found himself sitting on the verandah, a cup of tea in hand. The street outside buzzed with activity—children playing cricket, a vendor selling fresh vegetables, and neighbours exchanging pleasantries.

His mother joined him, carrying a tray of biscuits. "You know," she began, "when you were a boy, you always said you'd buy us a big house in the city. Do you still think about that?"

Vikram laughed softly. "Ma, I can barely keep up with my rent. A big house is still a long way off."

She smiled, but her eyes betrayed a hint of concern. "We don't need a big house, beta. We're happy here. But you... you work so hard. Do you ever stop to enjoy what you've achieved?"

The question caught him off guard. Had he? He thought about the promotions, the accolades, the long hours—and the loneliness that often accompanied them.

"I don't know," he admitted, looking down at his tea.

His mother reached over and patted his hand. "You should, beta. Life isn't just about running. Sometimes, it's about sitting still and enjoying the view."

Her words stayed with him long after she went back inside. Sitting still wasn't something he was used to. He had spent years chasing, striving, and pushing forward, but for what? And at what cost?

That evening, Vikram decided to take a walk around the neighbourhood. The streets felt smaller than he remembered, the houses more compact. Yet there was a charm in their familiarity—the same trees, the same shops, even the same old man sitting at the corner, watching the world go by.

As he passed a small park, he saw a group of teenagers practicing a dance routine. Their laughter echoed through the air, carefree and uninhibited. Vikram stopped to watch, their energy reminding him of his own youthful ambitions.

One of the boys noticed him and called out, "Bhaiya, want to join?"

Vikram chuckled. "I think I'm a little out of practice."

The boy grinned. "Practice makes perfect!"

The phrase struck a chord. It was something his college mentor had said to him during his first internship—a time when he had been brimming with enthusiasm, unburdened by the weight of expectations.

As Vikram walked back home, he realized how much he had changed since then. The dreams he once had, the passion that had fuelled him, had been replaced by a relentless pursuit of something he couldn't even name.

That night, as he packed his bag for the return journey, Vikram felt a strange mix of emotions. His parents had built a life rooted in simplicity and contentment, yet they had encouraged him to aim higher, to reach for the stars.

But was he really reaching, or was he just running? And if he was running, was it toward something, or away from something else?

As he zipped his suitcase shut, Vikram made a silent promise to himself: to find the answers, to rediscover the passion that had once defined him.

For the first time in months, he felt a flicker of hope.

VIII

The Unspoken Trade-Offs

The train ride back to the city was uneventful, but Vikram's mind was far from quiet. His mother's words echoed in his thoughts: *"Life isn't just about running."* The rhythmic clatter of the train wheels seemed to punctuate her message, as if urging him to slow down and reflect.

As the city skyline came into view, Vikram felt the familiar surge of adrenaline. The towering buildings, the endless rush of people, the hum of possibility—it was both exhilarating and exhausting. He checked his phone. Dozens of unread emails and a handful of missed calls awaited him.

By the time he reached his apartment, it was almost midnight. The suitcase landed in a corner with a dull thud, and Vikram collapsed onto the couch. He stared at the ceiling, letting the quietness of the moment wash over him.

What am I really chasing? he wondered.

The next morning, Vikram was back in the office, the hum of activity all too familiar. He had barely settled into his desk when Sameer, his colleague-turned-mentor, appeared with a cup of coffee in hand.

"Welcome back, traveller," Sameer said, sliding into the chair opposite him.

"Thanks," Vikram replied, his voice lacking its usual energy.

Sameer studied him for a moment. "You look... different. Trip didn't go as planned?"

"It was fine," Vikram said, shrugging. "Just got me thinking, that's all."

"Dangerous territory," Sameer joked, though his tone was kind. "What's on your mind?"

Vikram hesitated. Sameer had always been a good listener, but opening up wasn't something Vikram did easily. Still, the questions swirling in his mind felt too heavy to carry alone.

"Do you ever feel like we're all just running in circles?" Vikram asked.

Sameer leaned back, his expression thoughtful. "All the time. The trick is figuring out if the circle you're running is worth it."

"And how do you figure that out?"

Sameer smiled. "By asking yourself two questions: What are you running toward? And what are you running away from?"

The words hit Vikram like a punch to the gut. He had spent so much time focusing on the next target, the next milestone, that he hadn't stopped to consider what he was truly chasing—or avoiding.

Later that day, Vikram found himself in a meeting with the sales team. The room buzzed with nervous energy as the regional manager outlined the new quarterly targets. Charts and graphs filled the screen, each one more ambitious than the last.

"We're not just selling products," the manager declared. "We're selling solutions, dreams, possibilities. And the market is wide open—retail, software, real estate, you name it. We need to seize this moment."

Vikram glanced around the room. Some faces were alight with determination, while others wore thinly veiled expressions of doubt. He knew the pressure all too well—the endless expectations, the unspoken trade-offs.

After the meeting, one of the junior team members, Priya, approached him.

"Vikram, can I ask you something?" she said, her voice tinged with hesitation.

"Of course," he replied, motioning for her to sit.

"How do you… stay motivated? I mean, the targets keep growing, but it feels like no matter how much we achieve, it's never enough."

Vikram paused, unsure how to answer. He could offer a rehearsed line about perseverance or a cliché about passion, but he didn't want to. Instead, he said, "That's something I'm still figuring out myself."

Priya looked surprised but nodded. "Thanks. It's… nice to know I'm not the only one."

As she left, Vikram felt a pang of guilt. He wanted to be a source of inspiration, a guide for those just starting out. But how could he guide others when he was still lost himself?

That evening, Vikram sat at his desk, staring at his open journal. He began to write, his pen moving almost instinctively: *The unspoken trade-offs of ambition...*

He listed them one by one:

- Time with loved ones.
- Health, both physical and mental.
- The ability to enjoy small moments.
- A sense of purpose beyond the next target.

The list grew longer with each passing minute. By the time he set the pen down, the page was full. Vikram leaned back, the weight of his own words sinking in.

The next day, Vikram decided to take a different approach. Instead of diving straight into work, he spent the morning observing. He watched his colleagues, the way they interacted, the stories they carried behind their professional facades.

He noticed Rohit, the senior executive with a booming laugh, staring at a family photo on his desk, his smile tinged with longing. He saw Priya, her brow furrowed as she tried to make sense of an overwhelming spreadsheet. And then there was Sameer, always calm, always composed, but with a quiet melancholy in his eyes that spoke of sacrifices Vikram couldn't yet understand.

Each of them was running their own race, carrying their own burdens.

Maybe it's not about running faster or farther, Vikram thought. *Maybe it's about figuring out why we're running in the first place.*

IX

The Weight of Choices

The rain poured relentlessly, drumming against the glass panes of Vikram's office. The city was wrapped in a grey haze, its usual energy muted under the weight of the storm. Vikram stared at his reflection in the window, the outlines blurred and indistinct, much like his thoughts.

He glanced at his phone—a missed call from his mother and a notification from the bank about his latest loan instalment. Each one carried a different kind of urgency, a silent reminder of the choices he had made.

"Hcy, dreamer." Sameer's voice broke the silence. He walked in, holding two cups of chai.

"Thought you could use this," he said, placing one on Vikram's desk.

Vikram took the cup with a nod of thanks. The warmth seeped through his fingers, grounding him.

"You're unusually quiet today," Sameer observed.

"Just... thinking," Vikram replied, his voice trailing off.

Sameer leaned back in the chair, his gaze steady. "Thinking's good. Dangerous, but good. What's on your mind?"

Vikram hesitated. "Do you ever feel like the more choices you have, the heavier they get?"

Sameer's lips curled into a wry smile. "All the time. Choices are funny like that. They promise freedom but come with a cost."

"And what if you make the wrong one?"

Sameer took a sip of his chai, his expression contemplative. "There's no such thing as a wrong choice, Vikram. Just choices that teach you different lessons."

That evening, Vikram decided to confront one of his own choices—the one he had been avoiding for weeks. He picked up his phone and dialled a number he hadn't called in a long time.

"Vikram!" His mother's voice was warm, but there was an undertone of concern.

"Hi, Ma. How are you?"

"I'm fine, beta. But you sound tired. Are you eating properly?"

"I'm fine, Ma," he said, forcing a smile. "Just busy."

They talked for a few minutes, the conversation light but tinged with unspoken worries. Just as they were about to hang up, his mother said, "Vikram, do you remember the night before your engineering entrance exam?"

He frowned, surprised by the sudden shift in topic. "Of course. Why?"

"I remember you sitting at the table, your books spread everywhere, and saying, 'Ma, what if I don't get in? What if I fail?'" She paused, her voice softening. "And do you remember what I told you?"

Vikram did. *"It's not about the result. It's about the effort you put in."*

"I've been thinking about that a lot lately," he admitted.

"Beta, life is full of exams. Some you pass, some you don't. But the important thing is to keep going, to keep learning. That's all that matters."

Her words lingered in his mind long after the call ended.

The next day, Vikram found himself in the middle of a heated client negotiation. The stakes were high—landing the deal could open doors to a new market, but the client's demands were bordering on unreasonable.

"Mr. Kapoor, we're not just selling a product here," Vikram said, his tone calm but firm. "We're offering a partnership, a long-term solution that will benefit both sides. But that only works if it's fair."

The room fell silent. Vikram could feel the weight of every eye on him, the unspoken pressure to close the deal at any cost.

After what felt like an eternity, the client nodded. "You're right. Let's revisit the terms."

The meeting ended on a positive note, but Vikram felt no sense of triumph. Instead, he was struck by the complexity of the moment—the delicate balance between ambition and integrity, between saying yes and standing firm.

That night, as he walked home in the rain, Vikram's mind wandered to a memory from his childhood. He was eight years old, sitting on the steps of his house, watching his father repair an old transistor radio.

"Why are you fixing it, Papa?" he had asked. "Why not just buy a new one?"

His father had smiled, his hands steady as he worked. "Because, beta, some things are worth the effort. Not everything can be replaced."

The memory felt like a message, a quiet reminder of the values that had shaped him.

When Vikram reached his apartment, he opened his journal and began to write:

Choices are like rivers. Some flow smoothly, others are turbulent. But each one shapes the land it touches, leaving behind a story.

He thought about the choices that had brought him here—the decision to pursue a career in sales, the sacrifices he had made, the dreams he had deferred.

For the first time, he allowed himself to acknowledge both the pride and the pain of those choices.

X

The Art of Selling Dreams

The small café at the corner of the street was buzzing with chatter. The aroma of freshly brewed coffee mingled with the faint scent of rain-soaked earth. Vikram sat by the window, his notebook open, but his pen unmoving. The blank page stared back at him, as if challenging him to fill it.

Across the table, Ananya stirred her coffee, her movements deliberate. She was watching Vikram, her curiosity piqued by his silence.

"What's on your mind?" she finally asked.

He looked up, startled. "Just... trying to figure something out."

Ananya raised an eyebrow. "Must be something big if it has you this distracted."

Vikram leaned back, exhaling. "It's this question I can't shake off: What am I really selling? Is it the product, the promise, or the person I've become while selling it?"

Ananya's lips curled into a faint smile. "Maybe it's all three. Or maybe it's none. What do you think you're selling?"

Vikram hesitated. "Dreams, maybe? The idea that something better is just within reach if you make the right choice."

As the conversation lingered in his mind, Vikram found himself reflecting on a deal he had closed years ago, one that had stayed with him for reasons he couldn't quite explain.

It was his first major client—a young entrepreneur named Rahul who had just launched his own startup. Rahul had been hesitant, wary of promises that sounded too good to be true.

"Why should I trust you?" Rahul had asked, his eyes searching Vikram's for a hint of sincerity.

Vikram had taken a deep breath before replying. "Because I'm not just selling you a product. I'm selling you the belief that your vision is worth it, that it's possible to make it real. But that belief has to come from you first."

The deal had gone through, but it wasn't the commission that stayed with Vikram. It was the look on Rahul's face—a mix of hope and determination, as if he had just been handed the key to unlock his potential.

That evening, Vikram decided to put his thoughts into action. He organized a workshop for his team, titled *The Art of Selling Dreams.*

Standing before them, he began with a simple question: "What's the most important thing you've ever sold?"

The room buzzed with responses. "A luxury car." "A software package." "A house."

Vikram smiled, letting the answers settle. Then he asked, "And what did you really sell in those moments? Was it just the product?"

His team exchanged puzzled glances, unsure of where he was going.

"You sold trust," Vikram continued. "You sold possibility. You sold someone the courage to believe that what you were offering could change their life, even if just a little."

He paused, letting his words sink in. "And that's what makes this job so much more than a transaction. It's about connecting with people on a human level, understanding their hopes, fears, and aspirations."

Later that night, Vikram sat alone in his office, flipping through the notes his team had shared during the workshop. Each one told a different story—a struggling parent buying a laptop for their child's education, a newlywed couple purchasing their first car, a small business owner investing in software to expand their reach.

He realized that behind every sale was a dream, often unspoken but deeply felt.

Flashback: A Personal Sale

Vikram's mind drifted back to his childhood, to the time when his father had tried to sell the idea of education to him and his siblings. They had grown up in a modest home, where every rupee mattered.

"Why should we study so hard?" Vikram had once asked, frustrated by the endless hours of homework and tuition.

His father had looked at him, his eyes filled with a quiet intensity. "Because education is the only thing that can't be taken away from you. It's your ticket to a better life, to choices I never had."

Those words had stuck with him, shaping not just his career but his entire outlook on life.

The next day, Vikram found himself in another client meeting, this time with a middle-aged woman who ran a small bakery. She was hesitant about investing in a digital payment system, unsure if it was worth the expense.

Vikram listened patiently as she voiced her concerns. Then he said, "Do you know what I see when I look at your bakery?

I see a place where families celebrate birthdays, where friends catch up, where someone's day gets a little brighter because of your cakes.

This system isn't just about payments; it's about making those moments easier to create."

The woman's face softened, and Vikram knew he had connected with something deeper.

XI

The Weight of Expectations

The road ahead felt endless, yet the journey had only just begun. Rahul stood at the edge of the open balcony, his thoughts drifting into the night air. The cool breeze teased the edges of his shirt, but it wasn't enough to calm the storm inside his mind. The city below hummed with life—people hustling through their lives, unaware of the inner struggles that gripped others just like them. Yet, in this world of infinite distractions, Rahul's burden felt uniquely his own.

Earlier that evening, Rahul had left yet another high-stakes meeting, feeling a mixture of accomplishment and unease. The presentation had gone well—too well, in fact. His colleagues had applauded his efforts, praising him for the meticulous strategy he had presented. But beneath their words, he felt a gnawing discomfort. Was this what he had really wanted? To impress others with ideas that didn't quite resonate with his own values?

The office had emptied out quickly after the meeting, the usual chatter fading as everyone retreated to their own worlds. But Rahul lingered, sitting at his desk, the glow of his laptop screen illuminating his tired face. He glanced at the clock. It was nearly 9 p.m.

"Rahul, you're still here?" came a voice from the door. It was Priya, his colleague and friend, looking at him with concern. **"You really should go home. You've been at this all day."**

Rahul smiled weakly, leaning back in his chair. **"It's just one of those days. I'm not quite finished yet."**

Priya shook her head, taking a step into the office. **"You're always chasing something. I just hope you're chasing the right things."**

Her words lingered in the air as she left, but Rahul didn't have time to reflect on them immediately. He had deadlines to meet, calls to make, and the long list of tasks that stretched ahead of him like an unmovable wall. But deep down, he knew Priya had a point. Was he really chasing the right things? Was his path shaped by his own desires, or was it just the expectations of others pushing him forward?

He grabbed his jacket and walked out of the office, making his way toward the parking lot. His car was parked at the far end, the chill of the night air making him pull his collar up. As he reached the vehicle, his phone buzzed in his pocket. It was a message from his mother.

"How are you? Your father and I are waiting for you to visit this weekend. You've been working so hard. I hope you're taking care of yourself."

Rahul smiled bitterly. The words were kind, but they felt like another layer of pressure. She didn't understand. She didn't know what it was like to sit in endless meetings, to make decisions that impacted the lives of dozens of people, to be constantly on the clock, juggling client expectations and personal aspirations. She didn't know what it felt like to be 'successful' on the outside but feel completely lost inside.

When he finally reached home, Rahul sat by the window, his thoughts turning inward. He had always been taught that success was something tangible. His parents had never given him the luxury of defining success on his own terms. It was a well-charted course, a roadmap sketched long before his birth—finish school, get into the best college, land a high-paying job, climb the ladder, and find stability. Simple, right?

But life, Rahul soon realized, didn't adhere to any pre-determined plan. The corporate world was a labyrinth of demands, expectations, and pressures, none of which were visible in the glossy brochures or the polished LinkedIn profiles. And now, at this juncture, he had reached a critical threshold—a place where every step forward felt heavier than the last.

"Success," he mused, "was never meant to be a straight line. But why does it always feel like I'm racing against something?"

His mind wandered to the countless times he'd been told to 'hurry up and settle down,' to 'take the leap' and 'make something of yourself.' The expectations were unrelenting. It wasn't just his own ambitions that weighed on him, but those of his family, his friends, and even his colleagues. The expectation to always appear successful, to always have the answers, to keep climbing, to keep achieving.

Rahul often found himself wondering if anyone else felt the same way. If the polished suits and the confident smiles that people wore were just a façade, hiding the inner exhaustion they carried in silence. But in a world that celebrated achievement, was there room for failure? Could one openly admit that they were struggling without risking judgment?

He reached for his phone and checked his messages again. This time, it was a simple note from Priya. **"Don't be too hard on yourself. Remember, success isn't always about being perfect. Sometimes it's about knowing when to step back."**

Rahul took a deep breath, the weight of the day's events finally catching up to him. In the quiet of his apartment, he reflected on the journey so far. There was always a desire to prove himself, to show the world—and more importantly, his family—that he was worthy. Worthy of their sacrifices, worthy of the legacy of his father, worthy of the dreams they had for him. But somewhere along the way, that ambition had turned into obsession.

It was no longer about proving something to them, but about staying ahead of everyone else. The comparison was insidious, and it slowly took root in his psyche, pushing him further into a corner.

Now, sitting at the precipice of burnout, Rahul realized the toll this obsession had taken. The long hours, the constant pressure, the race to prove himself—all had led him to a place where he didn't know if he was pursuing a dream or merely surviving someone else's. The expectations, once motivating, had transformed into an unrelenting weight.

And yet, there was something inside him that refused to let go. Perhaps it was hope, or perhaps it was the fear of being left behind, but Rahul knew that this struggle, this balancing act between ambition and fulfilment, was not his alone. Every professional, from the small-time seller to the corporate titan, was battling a similar war—one fought in the silence of their minds, away from prying eyes.

He closed his eyes, taking a deep breath, letting the silence of the night settle over him. In that quiet moment, he didn't have to be the ambitious son, the high-flying executive, or the man with all the answers. He could simply be himself—a man who was learning, like everyone else, how to navigate the intricate web of expectations and identity.

XII

The Mirror Doesn't Lie

The early rays of dawn sliced through the thin curtains of Vikram's hotel room, painting the walls in hues of orange and gold. He stirred on the bed, half-covered by the white linen, his body weighed down by exhaustion. The suit jacket he had draped over a chair now slouched, mirroring his own state of mind.

The world outside was alive—the muffled honks of cars, the chatter of street vendors setting up their stalls. Yet, inside the room, time felt suspended. Vikram sat up, rubbing his temples. His head throbbed from the previous night's client dinner, where laughter and clinking glasses masked the anxiety of sealing the next big deal.

His eyes wandered to his reflection in the mirror across the room. There he was—Vikram, the successful executive with a trail of accolades, deals closed, and a reputation that preceded him. But as he looked closer, the reflection seemed distant, almost unfamiliar.

He got up and walked toward the mirror, standing inches away, searching for something—recognition, perhaps. The man staring back at him wore the same dark circles, the same stoic expression, and yet, Vikram couldn't help but feel like a stranger to himself.

The Morning Call

The shrill ring of his phone shattered the quiet. Vikram grabbed it from the bedside table, glancing at the screen: it was his father.

"Beta, how are you?" came the familiar voice, laced with warmth and concern.

"I'm fine, Papa," Vikram replied, forcing a smile as if his father could see through the phone.

"We haven't seen you in months. Your mother was saying... maybe you can come home this weekend?"

Vikram hesitated, glancing at the itinerary on his desk. A back-to-back schedule of meetings, calls, and travel stared back at him.

"I'll try, Papa. Things are a bit... hectic."

There was silence on the other end, a silence that spoke volumes. "Hectic is your life now, isn't it?" his father finally said, a tinge of disappointment in his voice.

Vikram closed his eyes, leaning against the desk. "I'll make time. Promise."

"Alright, beta. Just don't forget—this life, these successes, they mean little if you don't have people to share them with."

As the call ended, Vikram placed the phone down, staring at it as if it held the answers he desperately sought.

Breakfast with Rahul

Later that morning, Vikram found himself in the hotel's bustling restaurant. Rahul was already there, seated at a corner table with a plate of half-eaten toast and eggs. His younger colleague waved him over, his face lit up with youthful enthusiasm.

"Morning, Vikram! Slept well?" Rahul asked, though the question sounded rhetorical.

Vikram gave a non-committal nod as he slid into the seat opposite Rahul. A waiter approached, and Vikram ordered black coffee, his go-to remedy for sleepless nights.

"You know," Rahul began, his voice tinged with excitement, "I was thinking about what you said yesterday about focusing on the client's long-term goals. It's such a simple concept, but it's genius. I think I nailed it in the presentation."

Vikram managed a faint smile. "Good. The client's trust is everything."

Rahul leaned forward, his voice dropping to a conspiratorial whisper. "But honestly, Vikram, how do you do it? You're always so composed, always have the right answer. It's like you're ten steps ahead of everyone else."

Vikram paused, his fingers tracing the rim of his coffee cup. "You learn to mask the chaos, Rahul. That's all."

Rahul chuckled, taking it as a joke. "Well, whatever it is, it's inspiring."

The word "inspiring" hung in the air, making Vikram shift uncomfortably. He wanted to tell Rahul that it wasn't inspiration—it was survival. That the polished exterior came at a cost, a cost he wasn't sure he could keep paying.

The Quiet Encounter

After breakfast, Vikram stepped outside for a moment of solitude. The city stretched before him, alive and unapologetic. He leaned against the railing of the hotel's terrace, watching the chaos below.

A woman in her late forties stood a few feet away, holding a cup of tea. She looked out at the same view, a faint smile on her lips.

"Quite the city, isn't it?" she said, breaking the silence.

Vikram nodded. "Never stops moving."

She turned to him, her gaze sharp yet kind. "Neither do people like you, I suppose."

Vikram raised an eyebrow. "People like me?"

She chuckled. "The ones who carry the weight of the world on their shoulders. Always chasing, always achieving, but rarely stopping to breathe."

Her words struck a chord. "And what do you do?" he asked, curiosity piqued.

"I listen," she said simply. "And sometimes, I remind people that it's okay to pause."

Vikram stared at her, unsure of how to respond. But before he could ask more, she finished her tea and walked away, leaving him alone with her words.

The Reflection

That evening, as Vikram prepared for yet another flight, he found himself drawn back to the mirror. The stranger he had seen that morning was still there, but now, there was a flicker of something else—awareness, perhaps.

The woman's words echoed in his mind. "It's okay to pause."

For the first time in a long time, Vikram allowed himself to sit still, his thoughts tumbling out like an unorganized heap. The weight of expectations, the fear of failure, the relentless chase for recognition—it all felt heavy, yet strangely liberating to acknowledge.

As he closed his eyes, Vikram made a silent promise to himself. He would keep moving forward, yes, but he would also find moments to pause, to breathe, and to rediscover the man behind the reflection.

XIII

The Weight of Silence

The airport lounge buzzed with activity—an orchestra of hurried footsteps, rolling suitcases, and the occasional crackle of announcements. Vikram sat in a corner, cradling a steaming cup of chai. He had arrived early, not because he wanted to, but because being late added another layer of stress to his already cluttered mind.

He stared out of the glass façade, watching planes taxi along the runway. Each flight carried stories—people leaving, arriving, reuniting, or starting afresh. For Vikram, it was just another journey, another city, another deal.

His phone vibrated on the table. It was Priya.

"Safe travels," her message read, accompanied by a thumbs-up emoji.

He smiled faintly and typed back, "Thanks." But before he could hit send, he deleted it and set the phone aside. Words felt heavy today.

The Unexpected Encounter

"Mind if I sit here?"

The voice broke his reverie. Vikram looked up to see a man about his age, dressed in casual attire—jeans and a plaid shirt. His face carried a weathered charm, the kind that spoke of stories untold.

"Sure," Vikram said, gesturing to the seat across from him.

"Thanks. The lounge is packed," the man said, placing his laptop bag on the floor.

Vikram nodded politely, not particularly in the mood for small talk. But the man seemed undeterred by his silence.

"You traveling for work?"

"Yeah. You?"

"Same. Though I like to think of it as traveling for survival," the man said with a chuckle.

Vikram looked up, intrigued. "Survival?"

The man leaned back in his chair, a wistful smile playing on his lips. "I sell insurance. Not exactly the glamorous kind of job people dream about, but it keeps the lights on."

Vikram couldn't help but smirk. "Glamour is overrated."

"True," the man said, nodding. "Name's Ravi, by the way."

"Vikram."

They shook hands, and for a moment, the barriers of formality seemed to dissipate.

A Shared Moment

As the conversation unfolded, Ravi spoke freely, weaving stories of missed flights, sceptical clients, and the struggle of making people believe in something they often avoided thinking about—insurance.

"You know what's funny?" Ravi said, his tone light but his eyes serious. "We spend our lives convincing others to prepare for the worst, but we rarely prepare ourselves."

Vikram felt a pang of recognition. "True. It's easier to focus on others than on yourself."

Ravi studied him for a moment. "You seem like someone who's been running for a while."

The comment caught Vikram off guard. "Running from what?"

Ravi shrugged. "Only you can answer that."

Before Vikram could respond, the boarding announcement for Ravi's flight crackled through the speakers. Ravi stood, picking up his bag.

"Well, it was nice talking to you, Vikram. Good luck with... whatever you're running toward—or away from."

With a wave, Ravi disappeared into the crowd, leaving Vikram with his thoughts.

The Call Home

Later, as he waited for his own boarding call, Vikram found himself scrolling through his contacts. His thumb hovered over his mother's name. It had been weeks since he last spoke to her.

He hesitated, then pressed the call button.

"Hello, beta!" Her voice was warm, instantly soothing the frayed edges of his mind.

"Hi, Ma. How are you?"

"We're good. How are you? Eating properly? You sound tired."

Vikram chuckled softly. "I'm fine, Ma. Just work."

There was a pause, and then she said, "You know, your Papa and I were talking about you last night. He said you've become like a migratory bird—always on the move."

Her words were meant to be light, but they carried a weight that Vikram couldn't ignore.

"Ma... do you think I've changed?" he asked, surprising even himself with the question.

"Changed? Of course. Everyone changes, beta. But don't lose sight of yourself in the process."

As the call ended, Vikram leaned back in his chair, her words echoing in his mind.

The Reflection Continues

On the flight, Vikram found himself staring at his reflection in the window, the city lights below gradually fading into darkness.

Ravi's words, his mother's gentle concern—they all swirled in his mind, merging into a singular thought:

What am I running toward?

For the first time in years, he allowed himself to sit with the question, without trying to answer it.

XIV
Echoes of a Journey

The boarding gates bustled with activity, a microcosm of humanity in transit. Vikram stood near the large windows, his boarding pass in hand, observing the scene unfold like a silent movie. Airports had always fascinated him—their ability to compress countless lives, stories, and emotions into one shared space.

"Excuse me," a voice interrupted his thoughts.

Vikram turned to see an older man, perhaps in his late 50s, dressed in a simple white shirt and trousers. His face carried the weathered marks of a life lived in discipline, but his eyes sparkled with warmth.

"Mind if I sit here?" the man asked, gesturing to the seat beside Vikram.

"Of course, please," Vikram replied, moving his bag to make space.

A Conversation Unfolds

The man settled into the seat with a sigh, glancing at his watch. "These flight delays... they test your patience," he remarked with a chuckle.

Vikram nodded. "Happens all the time."

They sat in companionable silence for a moment before the man broke it. "Travel for work?"

"Yes. You?"

The man's smile faded slightly. "Family. My mother's in the hospital—emergency."

"I'm sorry to hear that. Is she going to be okay?"

"We're hopeful. She's tough—always has been," the man said, his voice carrying a blend of pride and worry.

As the conversation deepened, the man introduced himself as Captain Rajveer Singh, a retired officer from the armed forces. He spoke with an understated dignity about his years of service, the cities he had called home, and the life of constant movement that had defined him.

The Generational Reflection

"You know," Rajveer said, "I spent my entire career living out of a suitcase. And just when I thought I'd finally unpack for good, life had other plans. My daughter—she's following a similar path. Corporate job, endless travel, always on the move. I see a lot of myself in her, but sometimes I wonder... is this the life I wanted for her?"

Vikram leaned forward, intrigued. "What do you mean?"

Rajveer's eyes softened. "In the forces, I travelled because duty demanded it. But her travels—they're for ambition, for growth. It's different, yet the same. Both of us chasing something, but at what cost? I wonder if she feels the weight of it as I did."

The words hit Vikram like a quiet storm. He thought of his own relentless pursuit, the countless nights spent away from home, the silent sacrifices made in the name of progress.

The Call to Board

The boarding announcement for Rajveer's flight crackled over the speakers. The older man stood, adjusting the strap of his bag.

"It was nice talking to you, Vikram," he said, extending his hand.

"You too, Captain. And... I hope your mother gets better soon."

Rajveer nodded, a faint smile playing on his lips. "Thank you. Safe travels." As Vikram watched him disappear into the boarding queue, a thought lingered in his mind: **Are we all just reflections of the lives we've inherited, passing the same suitcase from one generation to the next?**

XV
Crossroads

The flight was uneventful, but Vikram's mind wasn't. The conversation with Captain Rajveer had planted a seed of restlessness in him, growing with each passing mile in the sky.

As he landed in yet another unfamiliar city, Vikram's senses were greeted by the now-familiar routine: the crisp air of the terminal, the distant hum of travellers' chatter, and the ever-present glow of fluorescent lights. But today, it all felt heavier. The suitcase he wheeled behind him seemed more than just a physical burden—it carried the weight of questions he wasn't ready to answer.

A Familiar Scene

By the time Vikram reached his hotel, the evening had begun to set in. He checked in with the mechanical precision of someone who had done it a thousand times before, nodding politely to the receptionist before making his way to his room.

The room was predictably sterile—neutral tones, spotless linens, a desk by the window. Yet, tonight, it felt almost mocking in its impersonality. Vikram dropped his suitcase in the corner and sank onto the bed, staring at the ceiling.

His phone buzzed. It was a text from his team lead: **"Don't forget the client meeting tomorrow. We need this one, Vikram."**

He tossed the phone aside. Work always loomed, demanding attention, pushing every other thought to the background. But tonight, he couldn't shake the feeling of being trapped in a cycle—a hamster wheel of endless meetings, deals, and fleeting rewards.

The Pull of Memory

Unbidden, memories of his childhood surfaced. Vikram saw himself as a young boy, sitting cross-legged on the floor of their modest home. His father, a small-town school teacher, would return home each evening, his shoulders drooping with exhaustion but his eyes alive with purpose.

"We do what we must, son," his father used to say, often over a simple meal of dal and roti. "So, you can do what you want one day."

Back then, those words had been his compass. They had propelled him through late-night study sessions, gruelling entrance exams, and the relentless pursuit of a career that promised stability and success. But now, as he sat in yet another rented room, he wondered: **Was this what he wanted?**

A Call from Home

His phone buzzed again. This time, it was his mother.

"Vikram, beta, how are you? Did you eat?"

Her voice was warm, a balm to his frayed nerves.

"Yes, Ma. Just landed. I'll eat in a bit," he replied.

"Good, good. You sound tired," she said, pausing before adding, "Take care of yourself, okay? You're working so hard... I just wish you didn't have to run around so much."

He smiled faintly. "It's part of the job, Ma. You know how it is."

"I know," she said, her voice softening. "But sometimes I wonder if this is the life we wanted for you when we pushed you to achieve more. You've done so much, Vikram, but... are you happy?"

The question hung in the air long after the call ended.

A Chance Encounter

Later that evening, Vikram decided to step out for a walk. The city streets were alive with a vibrancy that contrasted sharply with his own mood. He wandered aimlessly, eventually stopping at a roadside chai stall.

As he sipped the steaming tea, he noticed a young man standing nearby, engrossed in a conversation on his phone. The man, dressed in a sharp suit, was animated, gesturing emphatically as he spoke. Vikram couldn't help but catch snippets of the conversation: words like "targets," "deadlines," and "projections" floated through the air.

When the call ended, the man let out a deep sigh, leaning against the counter. "Long day?" Vikram asked, offering a small smile.

The man looked at him, startled, before chuckling. "Long life, more like."

They got to talking. The man, Aman, was a sales executive, juggling ambitious targets and a demanding boss. "It's funny," Aman said, "I got into this job thinking it would be a stepping stone. But now, it feels like the stone is on my chest."

The words struck a chord with Vikram. Here was someone at the beginning of his journey, already grappling with the same doubts and pressures that had taken Vikram years to acknowledge.

A Silent Resolution

As Vikram walked back to his hotel, he felt a strange mix of emotions. He thought of Captain Rajveer, of Aman, and of himself. Their stories were different, yet intertwined by the common threads of ambition, sacrifice, and the relentless pursuit of something just out of reach.

Back in his room, Vikram opened his laptop and began typing—notes, thoughts, questions. For the first time in a long while, he wasn't working on a presentation or a client proposal. Instead, he was writing for himself, trying to make sense of the life he had been living and the one he wanted to build.

"Are we all chasing success, or is success chasing us?" he typed, pausing to let the question linger on the screen.

XVI

A Glimpse of the Mirror

The train rocked gently, the rhythmic clatter of its wheels filling the air. Vikram sat by the window, staring at the endless fields blurring past. This wasn't a usual business trip or a client meeting. He was heading home—something he hadn't done in over a year. The reason wasn't celebration but obligation. His mother had called three times in the past week, her tone growing more insistent each time. "You've been away too long, beta. It's time you visited."

He couldn't ignore her anymore, but as the train sped closer to his hometown, unease gnawed at him.

The Arrival

The station was small, barely altered from the time Vikram had left for college years ago. A chaiwala called out to passengers, the aroma of freshly brewed tea mingling with the smell of coal smoke and oil from the idli vendor's cart. Vikram stood at the edge of the platform, scanning the crowd.

His father appeared, a faint stoop in his gait but his presence still commanding. Dressed in a crisp white kurta and carrying a battered leather bag, he walked toward Vikram with deliberate slowness.

"You've finally remembered us," his father said, half in jest, but his eyes betrayed a mixture of relief and reproach.

"It's been busy, Papa," Vikram replied, knowing how inadequate the words sounded.

Their conversation was sparse as they drove home in the family's aging Maruti. The roads were narrower than Vikram remembered, the trees denser. The small, quiet town moved at a pace that now felt alien to him.

Homecomings

As they pulled into the driveway, Vikram's mother rushed out, her face lighting up at the sight of him. She enveloped him in a hug, her thin frame surprisingly strong. The house smelled of freshly cooked dal and something sweet—kheer, he guessed.

At the dinner table, the family gathered. His younger sister Aarti, now married and visibly pregnant, teased him about his city ways. "Don't tell me you've forgotten how to eat with your hands, bhaiya."

The conversation flowed around him—updates about relatives, news from the town, and memories of shared moments from the past. Vikram smiled and nodded, but he felt like a visitor in his own home, disconnected from the intimacy that bound the others.

The Small Wins

Later that evening, as the family retired to their rooms, Vikram stepped out onto the veranda. The night was still, the stars scattered like glitter across the sky. He leaned against the railing, sipping a cup of chai his mother had made.

His father joined him, carrying his own cup. They stood in silence for a while, the unspoken tension between them stretching like a taut string.

"You've done well for yourself, Vikram," his father said eventually, his voice measured.

"Have I?" Vikram replied, a bitter edge creeping into his tone. "Sometimes it feels like I'm just running—chasing something I can't even define."

His father looked at him, his gaze steady. "That's the thing about success. It's like trying to fill a pot with a hole in the bottom. No matter how much you pour, it's never enough."

Vikram stared into his cup, the tea now lukewarm. "Then why do we chase it? Why do we sacrifice so much for something that doesn't satisfy us?"

His father smiled faintly. "Because the world tells us that's the only way to matter. But maybe it's time you asked yourself what really matters to you."

The Forgotten Roads

The next day, Vikram decided to take a walk through the town. He passed his old school, the playground where he'd played cricket with friends, and the corner shop where he'd spent his pocket money on orange-flavoured candy. Each step brought a memory, a fragment of a life he'd left behind.

At one point, he stopped at a small tea stall by the roadside, the same one he used to visit as a teenager. The chaiwala recognized him immediately.

"Vikram beta! It's been years!" the man exclaimed, his face breaking into a wide grin.

Vikram smiled, feeling a warmth he hadn't felt in a long time. As he sipped the steaming chai, he listened to the man recount stories of the town's changes. It was a simple moment, but it grounded Vikram in a way his high-rise apartment and corporate job never could.

That night, Vikram pulled out his journal—a habit he'd almost abandoned in recent months. He stared at the blank page, the pen hovering over it.

Finally, he wrote:

"Success isn't what I thought it would be. It's not the promotions, the paychecks, or the applause. It's the moments that make me feel alive—the chai on a quiet night, the laughter of family, the connection to something real. Maybe I've been looking in the wrong places all along."

As he closed the journal, he felt a strange sense of clarity. This trip home wasn't just a visit. It was a reminder of what he'd been missing—a mirror reflecting the parts of himself he'd forgotten.

XVII

The Fork in the Road

The early morning stillness was broken by the occasional chirping of birds. Vikram sat on the porch of his family home, sipping tea from a chipped ceramic cup. The steam curled upwards, dissolving into the crisp air. His eyes wandered across the narrow street, where neighbours bustled about, preparing for their day—a vendor arranging his cart, children chasing a stray ball, and an elderly couple strolling hand in hand.

This was a world Vikram had once known intimately, yet now it felt foreign, like a book he had read and forgotten.

The Unexpected Arrival

"Vikram! Come inside, beta," his mother called from the kitchen. Her voice, as warm as the smell of freshly fried puris, drew him back to reality.

Just as he stood, the rumble of a motorbike echoed through the lane. A young man dismounted, removing his helmet to reveal a familiar face.

"Rahul?" Vikram asked, his voice tinged with surprise.

Rahul, his younger cousin, strode towards him with an easy grin. "Surprised to see me? I had a feeling you'd need company today."

Vikram raised an eyebrow. "Company? For what?"

Rahul leaned against the porch railing. "For whatever's brewing in that overworked, restless head of yours."

A Walk Down Memory Lane

Rahul's unannounced visit quickly turned into a long walk through the town. The two stopped by the old tea stall where Vikram had spent countless evenings during his college days. The stall owner, an elderly man with a toothy grin, greeted Vikram warmly.

"Arre, sahab! It's been years. Still running the world, eh?"

Vikram managed a smile, but the words stung. Was he really running the world, or was the world running him?

As they sat on a wooden bench, Rahul spoke. "You know, Vikram bhaiya, everyone here thinks you've made it. Big job, big money, constant travel. But do *you* think you've made it?"

Vikram stared at his tea. "I don't know. Sometimes, I feel like I'm just moving, not progressing. There's this... void."

Rahul nodded. "A void you've been running from. That's why you travel so much, isn't it? You're not searching for success; you're searching for purpose."

The Family Dinner

That evening, the entire family gathered for dinner. The dining table, laden with steaming dishes, became a hub of laughter and chatter. Stories of childhood pranks and old arguments flowed freely.

At one point, Vikram's father, usually a man of few words, spoke up. "Vikram, do you remember the time you spent an entire summer helping the local kids build a cricket pitch?"

Vikram laughed. "I do. We even painted stumps on the wall of the school!"

His father smiled. "You were so determined to create something lasting. That's the Vikram I remember—the one who cared more about impact than titles."

The room fell silent, the weight of his father's words settling over the table.

A Night of Reflection

Later that night, Rahul found Vikram sitting on the terrace, staring at the stars.

"You okay?" Rahul asked, settling beside him.

"I don't know," Vikram admitted. "Being here, hearing everyone's stories, it's making me question everything. Am I chasing the right things? Or am I just... lost?"

Rahul placed a hand on his shoulder. "You're not lost, bhaiya. You're just at a crossroads. And that's okay. The important thing is to figure out which road leads you closer to the person you want to be."

Vikram nodded, the notebook his mother had given him resting in his lap. Slowly, he opened it and began to write.

The Fork in the Road

The next morning, Vikram stood by the gate, bags packed, ready to leave. His mother hugged him tightly. "Remember, beta, no matter where you go, this will always be home."

As the car pulled away, Vikram glanced back at the house, his family waving from the porch. In his pocket, the notebook felt heavier than before, as if it carried not just blank pages but the weight of his choices.

This wasn't just a return to the city. It was the beginning of a new chapter—not just in his life, but in how he understood himself and the journey ahead.

XVIII
The Echo of Choices

The city skyline was shrouded in a thin layer of fog as Vikram's cab wove through the morning traffic. The chaos of honking cars and street vendors yelling their wares contrasted sharply with the tranquillity he had left behind at home. His mind, however, was anything but tranquil. The words of his father and Rahul echoed in his thoughts, challenging him to confront questions he had long avoided.

Back to the Grind

The office greeted him with its usual hum of activity—keyboards clattering, phones ringing, and colleagues rushing between meetings. Vikram moved through it all like a man underwater, his movements slow and deliberate as if the weight of his reflections from home had followed him.

His assistant, Priya, appeared at his desk with a pile of files. "Good morning, sir. The client presentation is scheduled for 3 PM, and the team has a review at 11. Also, there's a mail from HR about the leadership summit next week."

"Thanks, Priya," Vikram said, barely looking up.

As she left, he opened his laptop and stared at the calendar filled with back-to-back meetings. For the first time, the packed schedule felt suffocating rather than fulfilling.

The Meeting That Changed Everything

At 11 sharp, Vikram walked into the meeting room. The team was already assembled, discussing strategies for a product pitch. Rahul's words from the tea stall replayed in his head: *"You're not searching for success; you're searching for purpose."*

As the discussion progressed, Vikram noticed a recurring theme—targets, profits, and deadlines. No one spoke about the people behind the numbers, the customers whose lives they aimed to touch.

Interrupting the flow, Vikram asked, "What's the story we're selling here? Why would someone buy this product, beyond the price or features?"

The room fell silent. A junior team member, Ananya, hesitated before speaking. "Sir, isn't the story just about making lives easier? That's why I joined this project—to create something meaningful."

Her words hit Vikram like a thunderbolt. *When was the last time I worked on something meaningful?*

A Conversation with Sameer

Later that evening, Vikram called Sameer, an old friend and mentor who had a knack for asking the right questions.

"Sameer, do you ever feel like you're running on a treadmill? Moving fast but going nowhere?" Vikram asked, his voice tinged with frustration.

Sameer chuckled. "Welcome to the club, my friend. The question isn't whether you're running; it's why you're running."

Vikram leaned back in his chair. "I don't know anymore. I thought climbing the corporate ladder was the answer, but now it feels... hollow."

"That's because ladders don't lead to fulfilment. They lead to ceilings," Sameer said. "You need to ask yourself, what's the *ceiling* you're willing to stop at? And is it worth it?"

The call ended with Vikram more unsettled than ever, but also more determined to find answers.

The Notebook Beckons

That night, Vikram sat by his window, the city lights flickering in the distance. He pulled out the notebook his mother had given him and flipped through the blank pages.

What am I chasing? he wrote at the top of the first page.

Memories of his childhood ambitions, his first job, and the countless sacrifices he had made over the years spilled onto the paper. The words were raw and unfiltered, a stream of consciousness that revealed more than he had expected.

The Decision

By the time he closed the notebook, the first light of dawn was breaking through the skyline. Vikram felt a strange sense of calm, as if the act of writing had unburdened him. He wasn't sure what his next steps would be, but for the first time in years, he felt ready to ask the hard questions.

As he walked to the balcony, a line from his father's dinner table conversation came back to him: *"You cared more about impact than titles."*

Perhaps it was time to rediscover that part of himself.

XIX

In the Trenches

Vikram's days in the office were beginning to feel increasingly detached from reality. The polished presentations, meticulously crafted emails, and carefully curated meetings all seemed to miss the pulse of what was truly happening in the market.

Sameer had always said, "If you want to understand the value of what you do, step into the shoes of those who make it happen."

Taking that advice to heart, Vikram decided to spend a week on the field, shadowing the very people who were the backbone of the company—its sales force.

The First Day: A Roadside Reality

Monday morning found Vikram standing at a bustling market square, waiting for Arjun, one of the company's most seasoned sales executives. The air was thick with the aroma of spices and fried snacks, mingling with the cacophony of street vendors and honking cars.

Arjun arrived, a worn-out satchel slung over his shoulder. His enthusiasm was infectious despite the early hour.

"Sir, welcome to the ground. Ready for the real action?" Arjun said with a grin.

Their first stop was a tiny electronics shop tucked between a pharmacy and a tea stall. The shopkeeper, a middle-aged man with a stern expression, listened as Arjun made his pitch for the latest product line.

Vikram watched silently, observing the dynamics of the conversation. Arjun's tone was respectful yet persuasive, his arguments tailored to the shopkeeper's needs. Yet, the deal didn't close.

"Margins are too low," the shopkeeper said curtly before turning away.

As they walked out, Arjun shrugged. "This is how it is. You win some, you lose some. But you never stop trying."

The Long Walks

By noon, Vikram's feet ached from walking through narrow lanes and climbing stairs in unremarkable buildings. Each meeting brought a new challenge: price negotiations, delivery issues, or a competitor's undercutting tactics.

At one shop, the owner openly berated Arjun for a delayed shipment. Vikram cringed, expecting Arjun to retaliate, but the salesperson stayed calm, apologized, and promised to resolve the issue personally.

As they left, Vikram asked, "How do you handle that without losing your cool?"

Arjun smiled wryly. "If I take it personally, I'll burn out by lunchtime. You have to understand, they're running a business too. It's never about you; it's about their trust in the system."

A Night at the Tea Stall

After a gruelling day, Vikram and Arjun stopped at a roadside tea stall for a quick break. The tea, served in small clay cups, tasted better than anything Vikram had sipped in his corporate office.

Arjun shared stories of his journey—late-night bus rides, missed family events, and moments of doubt. "You know, sir, people think sales is just about targets and commissions. But it's more than that. It's about building relationships, even if they don't always work out. That's what keeps me going."

As the tea vendor cleared their cups, Vikram realized how disconnected he had been from the challenges faced by people like Arjun.

The Struggle of Rejection

By the third day, Vikram was beginning to grasp the emotional toll of rejection. At one meeting, a promising client dismissed Arjun's efforts entirely, leaving both men deflated.

"Do you ever feel like giving up?" Vikram asked as they walked back to the car.

Arjun paused, then said, "Many times. But then I remember why I started. It's not just about the job; it's about providing for my family, about proving to myself that I can do this."

The words stayed with Vikram.

The Silent Observations

On Friday, Vikram accompanied Priya, another salesperson, to a posh corporate office. Watching her navigate the meeting, he noted how different her approach was from Arjun's. While Arjun relied on relationships, Priya used data and insights to make her case.

The client, a young executive, was impressed but hesitant. "We're already in talks with someone else. Why should we choose you?"

Priya didn't miss a beat. "Because we don't just sell products; we sell solutions tailored to your needs. Here's how we've done it for others in your industry."

The deal closed that afternoon.

The Lessons Learned

By the end of the week, Vikram was exhausted but enlightened. He had witnessed the grit, resilience, and creativity of the sales force. He saw their struggles—the long hours, the relentless rejections—and their triumphs, however small.

Back in his office, Vikram looked at the framed awards on his desk. They felt hollow now, mere symbols of achievements that didn't capture the reality of what he had just experienced.

He opened his notebook and wrote:

"Sales isn't just about numbers; it's about people. It's about understanding their needs, their struggles, and their dreams. And in doing so, finding a piece of yourself."

Vikram knew he was only beginning to scratch the surface, but for the first time, he felt a sense of clarity.

XX
The Threshold of Change

Vikram sat in his hotel room, staring out at the city lights blinking in the distance. The world outside seemed distant, almost as if it belonged to someone else. He had experienced another long day—this time spent shadowing Arjun, a sales representative from a local furniture company. Their journey through the city's crowded streets, door-to-door visits, and relentless rejections had left him drained, both physically and mentally. But there was something else now, a quiet shift deep within him that he couldn't quite place.

Vikram was used to managing from a distance—watching others work, making decisions, and offering advice from the safety of a comfortable office. But today, he had been in the trenches. He had felt the weight of rejection as Arjun had, witnessed the disappointment in his eyes after every "no," and shared in the small victories when a potential customer showed interest.

He had seen firsthand the complexities of the job—the long hours, the unpredictability, and the emotional toll it took. It wasn't just about closing sales; it was about navigating personal lives, managing expectations, and dealing with the unseen pressures that no one ever spoke about.

Vikram's mind kept drifting back to Priya, the young woman he had met earlier that day at a café. She had been a breath of fresh air—a recent college graduate who had chosen to work in sales despite all odds. When she spoke about her dreams of becoming a leader in the sales industry, Vikram had been struck by the fire in her eyes. But as they spoke further, he realized how much she was trying to prove herself, not just to her family or society, but to herself. She, like so many others, was running from something—running toward success, toward acceptance, toward validation.

The conversation with Priya had reminded him of his own journey—the endless chase for validation that had once consumed him. Now, after witnessing the raw struggles of the people he had once considered mere numbers, Vikram found himself questioning everything he had built his career upon.

In that moment, Vikram understood something fundamental. Leadership, success, and fulfilment couldn't be achieved by merely checking boxes or following a predetermined path. True leadership came from understanding the complexities of those you led—their struggles, their joys, and the quiet battles they fought within themselves.

His phone buzzed, pulling him out of his thoughts. A message from Rahul.

"Hope today was eye-opening. You're beginning to see things differently now, aren't you?"

Vikram stared at the message for a long time, a small smile tugging at the corners of his mouth. Rahul had always been perceptive, always able to sense when Vikram was on the verge of a breakthrough. He typed a quick reply.

"I think I'm starting to understand what it really takes."

The message was simple, but it carried a weight that Vikram hadn't anticipated. He wasn't just talking about sales anymore. He was talking about life, about the journey he had been on, and the journey he was about to embark upon. This was no longer about chasing numbers or securing deals. It was about connecting with people on a deeper level—understanding their fears, their aspirations, and, most importantly, their humanity.

Vikram leaned back in his chair, his gaze still fixed on the skyline. The city stretched out before him, a sprawling testament to ambition, struggle, and possibility. But now, it felt different. It felt like a place where every individual was carrying a story, a weight, a dream.

And in that realization, Vikram knew that his own story was far from over. This was just the beginning.

XXI

The Shift Within

Vikram had always been a man of structure. A planner. A strategist. His career had been built on the firm belief that results could be predicted, systems could be controlled, and success could be mapped out with precision. But now, sitting in the corner of yet another hotel room—this one in a city far from home—he couldn't help but reflect on how little control he had over his own journey.

His phone buzzed again, this time with a message from Rahul, his quiet mentor and friend.

"You seem different today. You're at a crossroads, aren't you?"

Vikram's fingers hovered over the keyboard for a moment. How could he explain what was happening inside him? How could he articulate the subtle shift that had taken place over the last few weeks? How the world had slowly unravelled and revealed itself to him in a way that was both overwhelming and liberating?

He typed, then deleted, his response several times before finally sending:

"I'm not sure anymore, Rahul. Everything's changing. I feel like

I'm on the edge of something important, but I don't know what."

There was a pause before Rahul's reply came in.

"That's exactly it. You're beginning to see the real journey now. The one that can't be plotted on a map. You'll figure it out."

Vikram stared at the message, his mind swirling. He had always prided himself on knowing the next move, on understanding how to take the next step. But now, for the first time in years, he felt uncertain.

He thought about his conversation with Priya the previous day. She had been so sure of her goals, so certain that a career in sales was her way out of the struggle, the key to the life she wanted. Vikram envied her conviction, even as he saw the cracks beneath her confidence. He had seen it before—people who chased success because they believed it would fill a void they didn't fully understand.

But Vikram was no longer in a rush to chase that success. He wasn't sure if he even wanted it the way he used to.

There was a knock at the door. It was the hotel staff, bringing his late dinner. The small moment broke his train of thought, and for a moment, he simply breathed, feeling the weight of the room around him. There was no urgency now. No pressure to be anywhere. No ticking clock.

As he sat down to eat, he thought about the long days he had spent shadowing salespeople. How, over the course of the last few weeks, he had learned more about the realities of sales than he had in all his years of corporate leadership. He had seen the exhaustion, the frustration, the quiet persistence that kept people going despite constant setbacks. And he had seen the reward in their eyes—the satisfaction of a job well done, even when the result wasn't what they had hoped for.

What would it take for him to feel that way? To find meaning in the small victories?

Vikram knew now that success couldn't be measured by the numbers or the titles. It had to be measured by the depth of his connections with people, by the moments when he truly understood their needs and challenges, and by the choices he made from a place of integrity, not fear.

He thought back to his earlier reflections about leadership. How leadership, he had believed, was about guiding others to achieve great things. But what if true leadership wasn't about directing people toward a destination? What if it was about walking beside them on their journey, offering support, understanding, and encouragement, without forcing them into a mould?

For the first time in a long while, Vikram felt a deep sense of peace settle within him. He didn't have all the answers, but he was finally beginning to understand that he didn't need to. He didn't have to know the destination if he was willing to embrace the journey itself.

As he finished his meal and turned off the lights, he felt a quiet excitement building within him.

There was a world outside the windows of his hotel room—a world of possibility, of growth, of connection. And he was no longer afraid to face it.

Tomorrow, he would step into it differently. With less certainty about where he was going, but with a deeper understanding of why he was going at all.

XXII

The Ripple Effect

Vikram entered the conference room, greeted by the usual sea of faces, all waiting for his analysis and insights. He'd spent weeks meeting with the sales team, working closely with them in the field, and what he had seen—what he had experienced—had started to shift his perspective.

The data on the screen didn't tell the real story. These numbers were not just figures—they were people, striving, struggling, and persevering through inefficiencies that went unnoticed at the top.

Vikram's time on the ground had given him a new lens on leadership. The constant delays, the slow approval processes, and the fragmented communication were like cracks in the foundation of the company's operations. The effect was far-reaching, impacting not just sales, but morale.

He spoke slowly, each word deliberates. "We're looking at more than just sales numbers here. These numbers represent real people—people who are doing their best every day with the tools we've given them."

His eyes scanned the room, noticing how the words were beginning to resonate. He wasn't lecturing on corporate strategies or revenue forecasts. He was acknowledging the reality of the situation.

"We've been focusing on the wrong things," Vikram continued. "Efficiency doesn't come from complicated strategies or micromanagement. It comes from understanding the process, identifying where the system fails, and fixing those leaks."

The team members exchanged looks. Vikram wasn't asking for drastic changes. He wasn't looking for grandiose ideas. He was asking for simple improvements that could streamline their work and get them the support they needed, faster.

"The slow approval processes are killing us," Priya, a seasoned member of the team, spoke up. "By the time we get approval, the deal is gone. We lose momentum, and the client goes elsewhere."

Vikram nodded, absorbing the weight of her words. This was where the leaks were. He could see it now. The delays were tiny at first, but over time, they compounded, costing the company more than just lost deals—they were costing them trust, credibility, and the opportunity to build stronger relationships with clients.

"What if we empower our team to approve small discounts on their own?" Vikram suggested. "Let's remove the bottlenecks. Give them the tools and trust they need to close deals in real time."

The room fell silent for a moment. Then, one by one, team members began nodding. A wave of understanding passed through them. They weren't just going to be given more work or more directives. They were going to be trusted with responsibility.

Vikram smiled. He had found the way forward. Fixing the leaks wasn't about overhauling everything—it was about addressing the simple things that mattered, one step at a time.

XXIII

The Power of
Empowerment

The changes Vikram had discussed in the meeting were already beginning to take shape. Over the next few weeks, he worked tirelessly alongside his team to streamline the processes that had been hindering their progress. He spent time listening to the challenges the team was facing, identifying inefficiencies, and working with them to implement changes.

Priya's idea of allowing reps to approve discounts on their own had gained traction, and the early results were promising. Deals were closing faster, and the frustration that had once been so palpable in the team's conversations was now starting to fade.

But one afternoon, as Vikram sat in his office, a thought crossed his mind: Trust alone wasn't enough. Empowerment meant more than just giving people the ability to make decisions. It meant creating an environment where those decisions could be executed quickly and effectively.

The real challenge wasn't the approval process. It was the support system behind those decisions.

Empowerment, Vikram realized, had to be about creating a seamless path from decision to action.

He began working with the operations team to ensure that the sales reps had everything they needed to follow through with their decisions. It wasn't enough for them to make a call on the spot—once they did, the resources, tools, and support had to be in place to help them execute.

He wanted to ensure that the team wasn't just given responsibility without the means to carry it out.

One afternoon, Vikram walked into the office and noticed Arjun, a young rep, looking frustrated as he stared at his laptop. Vikram approached him and asked what was wrong.

"The discount system—it's not working. I'm trying to apply the discount, but it keeps rejecting it," Arjun said, clearly exasperated.

Vikram didn't brush him off. Instead, he sat beside Arjun and asked him to walk through the process step by step. As Arjun explained the issue, Vikram realized that a small glitch in the system was preventing the new approval process from being executed.

"Let's fix that," Vikram said, dialling the IT department.

Within hours, the issue was resolved, and Arjun was able to complete the sale smoothly.

It was a small fix, but it made a world of difference.

Arjun felt empowered—he had made a decision, and he had the tools to follow through. The delay had been frustrating, but now the road ahead was clear. Vikram smiled, knowing that the changes were taking root.

XXIV

The Last Mile

The real work, Vikram soon learned, wasn't just in empowering people to make decisions. It was about ensuring those decisions were carried out effectively.

As he spent more time working with his team, he realized that many decisions fell flat simply because they weren't executed well. There was always something in the way: miscommunication, lack of follow-through, or inadequate resources. But the key to success wasn't just in giving people the authority to make decisions—it was in making sure those decisions were carried through to the last mile.

Vikram spent a significant amount of time ensuring that the systems they had put in place were working smoothly. He followed up with sales reps to ensure that the tools and resources they needed were accessible and that any issues they encountered were resolved quickly.

His focus wasn't just on the big picture—it was on the small details that made a difference in the field. He met with reps to hear about their challenges and make sure their feedback was being implemented. Every issue, no matter how small, was addressed with urgency. Vikram wasn't satisfied until the team had the support they needed to execute on their decisions.

One evening, as Vikram walked through the office, he overheard a conversation between a couple of sales reps. They were discussing a recent deal they had closed, and how easy it had been to finalize it now that the approval process had been streamlined.

"You know," one of them said, "I can't remember the last time I felt this confident about a sale. Things are moving faster, and I don't have to wait for weeks to close a deal. I can do it on the spot."

Vikram's heart swelled with pride. It wasn't just about the process or the systems—it was about the people. They were becoming empowered, and that was the true success.

XXV
Leading with Clarity

The changes Vikram had implemented were having the desired effect. Sales were improving, but more importantly, the team had started to flourish. They felt supported, they felt trusted, and most importantly, they felt empowered to make decisions that drove results.

But Vikram knew that leadership wasn't just about fixing broken systems. It was about creating a culture of trust, respect, and support. It was about understanding that true leadership meant giving your team the tools and resources they needed to succeed and then getting out of their way to let them do their best work.

As Vikram sat at his desk one quiet evening, reviewing the latest numbers, he realized that leadership wasn't just about strategy. It was about people. It was about enabling them to do their best work and then standing back and letting them shine.

He smiled, knowing that his journey had only just begun.

Moment of Clarity

Vikram sat alone in the dimly lit coffee shop, his fingers absentmindedly tracing the rim of his mug. The noise of the city outside seemed to fade as he sunk deeper into his thoughts. The past few months had felt like a whirlwind of experiences, encounters, and internal reckonings. But now, in this rare moment of stillness, he found himself confronted with the question he had been avoiding for so long: *What now?*

His journey had taken him from the comfortable cocoon of corporate success to the messy, unpredictable world of hands-on work. He had tasted both failure and triumph, each shaping him in ways he hadn't anticipated. But as he sat here, away from the chaos of daily life, he realized there was something that had been missing—the full integration of his professional and personal identities. For too long, he had kept them separate, compartmentalized, as if his career could exist in isolation from the rest of his life.

The people he met on his travels, the friends he had made, the mentorship he had received—each one had left an imprint on him, but it wasn't enough. He hadn't yet learned the full lesson. The realization hit him in a wave: *It's not just about success. It's about the meaning behind that success.*

As he reflected, a memory surfaced. The conversation with his old mentor, Ramesh, a few months ago, had stirred something deep within him. "Vikram, it's never about the destination," Ramesh had said, leaning back in his chair, his eyes narrowing with a knowing smile. "It's about how you show up every single day, how you face the struggles, and how you stay grounded when everything around you changes."

The words echoed in Vikram's mind as the weight of their truth settled in. The external success, the accolades, the promotions—they were just markers. What truly mattered was how he felt inside, how he approached the work, and how he impacted those around him. This moment of clarity was exactly what he needed.

But the journey ahead would not be easy. It required something deeper—a commitment to alignment between who he was and what he did. And in that moment, Vikram understood what he needed to do next. He wasn't just going to focus on climbing the ladder anymore. He was going to build something more meaningful, something that would leave an imprint on others, on the people who looked up to him.

His heart pounded with a new sense of purpose as the next steps formed in his mind. This wasn't just about doing more work; it was about doing the right work. The work that resonated with his values and the people around him. The work that made a difference.

The realization brought a sense of peace. There would still be challenges ahead, of course, but Vikram was no longer afraid of them. He was ready to face the future, equipped not only with his professional skills but with the understanding that success could mean something far deeper than he had ever imagined.

XXVI

The Weight of Unseen Struggles

Vikram sat on the balcony of his small apartment, the city lights flickering like distant stars. It was late, and the quiet hum of the city below seemed to mirror the thoughts swirling in his head. He had just finished another gruelling day—a mix of client meetings, strategy sessions, and the endless stream of emails. The world outside his office felt distant, yet the pressure of his professional commitments had a gravitational pull that kept him tethered to it.

He often wondered how much of this he truly wanted. Was this success? Or was it an obsession, a constant race to prove himself, to fulfil expectations that were never his own? He remembered the words his father had once said: *"Success isn't just about what you achieve; it's about how you balance it with everything else."*

Balance. That word seemed so far from his reality. His family had always supported him, but the strain was visible. His wife's worried glance when he mentioned another late night at work, the missed dinners with his children—these were the small things he had brushed aside, telling himself they were temporary sacrifices for a bigger goal. But somewhere in the depths of his heart, Vikram knew that the cost of his obsession was higher than he was willing to admit.

He thought back to a recent conversation with his daughter. She had asked, *"Daddy, why are you always working? Are you ever coming home early?"* Her words, innocent yet piercing, had cut through the layers of justification he had built around his life. How had he gotten so consumed by his work that he couldn't even remember the last time he had truly been present with his family?

As he reflected, he saw a pattern—a pattern that many professionals in his circle followed, one that he had blindly embraced: the obsession with success, the drive to prove oneself at the expense of personal connections. It wasn't just about reaching the top; it was about staying there, no matter the cost.

His mind wandered to the faces of those he had met on his journey—his colleagues who pushed their limits daily, their families who silently bore the brunt of their professional pursuits. The weight of ambition was heavy, but it was often invisible, hidden beneath the veneer of success and the relentless pursuit of more.

Vikram leaned back in his chair, taking a deep breath. The obsession wasn't just about the work itself; it was about the validation, the recognition, the need to constantly prove that he was worthy of the life he had created.

But at what cost?

In the silence of the night, Vikram came to a painful realization.

His obsession was a double-edged sword. While it had propelled him to great heights, it was also taking away from the very things that mattered most. His family. His health. His peace of mind.

XXVII

The Toll of Obsession on Relationships

The following morning, Vikram woke up to the sound of his phone buzzing relentlessly. Another day, another set of meetings, another round of decisions to make. But as he sat up in bed, he found his mind wandering to the conversation he had had the previous night. He had not yet spoken to his wife, Aarushi, about his reflections. They had been drifting apart, each caught in their own whirlwind of commitments, never finding the time to truly connect.

Vikram knew that he needed to address the growing distance between them. But how? The weight of his professional commitments had made him a stranger in his own home, and no amount of success could ever make up for the emotional void he had created.

The moment he walked into the kitchen, Aarushi greeted him with a tired smile, her eyes betraying the exhaustion she had been carrying. The silence between them was thick, laden with unspoken words.

"Aarushi," Vikram began, his voice tentative, "I've been thinking about what you said yesterday... about how I'm always working. I realize I've been distant."

Aarushi looked at him, her gaze searching for sincerity. "Vikram, I know you're working hard. But what about us? What about the moments we're losing? The time with the kids, the weekends that slip away? We're both so busy, but at what cost?"

Her words hit him like a punch in the stomach. He had been so absorbed in his work, in the pursuit of success, that he had failed to notice how much of a toll it was taking on his family. The endless meetings, the business trips, the late nights—it had all come at the expense of the moments that truly mattered.

"I'm sorry, Aarushi. I didn't realize how much I was neglecting you and the kids. I've been so obsessed with proving myself, with achieving more, that I forgot about what's right in front of me."

Aarushi's expression softened, but there was still a sadness in her eyes. "It's not just about the apology, Vikram. It's about the change.

Can we find a way to balance it all? To make space for each other?"

Vikram nodded, the weight of the question settling heavily in his chest. He knew that the journey ahead would not be easy.

It would require sacrifices, compromises, and a willingness to let go of his obsession with success in favour of something more meaningful.

As he stood there, looking at his wife, he realized that this was the most important battle he had yet to face—the battle between his obsession and the relationships that defined his life.

It was a battle he could no longer afford to lose.

XXVIII

The Unseen Threads

Vikram sat at his desk, the soft hum of his laptop blending with the distant sounds of a bustling office. The day had started like any other—an endless stream of emails, calls, and meetings. But today, something felt different. The usual pace, the flurry of activity that once fuelled his every move, now seemed distant, almost irrelevant.

It was in the quiet moments, like now, when he began to reflect on the subtle shifts that had occurred over the years. The years of chasing success, the long hours, the countless sacrifices, all of it had led him to this point. Yet, the deeper he looked, the more it became clear—he had been chasing something external, something that could never truly satisfy.

He thought of his family, especially his wife, Aarushi, who had always been the steady presence in his life. She had supported him through it all—the late nights, the missed birthdays, the vacations that never happened. Yet, despite her unwavering support, there had always been a certain distance between them, a quiet understanding that she had accepted his "obsession," but had never fully embraced it.

As he sat there, a thought crossed his mind: *What if this obsession wasn't really about success?* What if it was about proving something to himself, to others, to the world? But more importantly, what if he could let go of it? Let go of the need to constantly prove his worth, to live up to an ideal that wasn't truly his.

The words of his mentor, Sameer, echoed in his mind:

"Success is not in the destination, Vikram. It's in the journey. The real victory lies in knowing that you've done your best, that you've given everything you had, and that you can walk away with peace in your heart."

For the first time in years, Vikram found himself questioning everything. Was his family paying the price for his obsession? Was the relentless pursuit of success worth the cost of time, of meaningful moments that he would never get back?

He closed his eyes, letting the silence fill him. The soft rhythm of his breath, the stillness in the room—it all felt foreign yet familiar. He had never allowed himself to pause like this before, never allowed himself the luxury of introspection.

But this was different. This was the moment of reckoning, the quiet realization that what he had been searching for was never out there—it was always within him.

The journey wasn't about building a legacy through numbers or accolades. It was about the people who had supported him, the quiet moments shared with his family, the laughter, the conversations, the fleeting glances that spoke volumes.

Vikram stood up, stretching his stiff legs. He walked to the window and looked out, his mind racing with the realization that he had a choice. A choice to redefine success on his own terms. A choice to prioritize what truly mattered.

He thought of the younger generation—the ones who, unlike him, were redefining what success meant. Talent, creativity, and capabilities were becoming the new currency, not the years spent climbing a hierarchical ladder. Vikram had seen young professionals rise to leadership roles, not because of their age or experience but because of their skill, their vision, and their ability to make decisions that mattered. The world was changing. The obsession with waiting for age and experience to dictate roles was fading away.

This realization hit him hard. *What if the old concept of "paying your dues"—putting in years of work to earn a decision-making role—was now obsolete?*

Young people today weren't just looking for success. They were seeking purpose, impact, and a sense of autonomy from an earlier age.

Companies were recognizing this shift, and Vikram could see how the corporate world was starting to evolve—young talent was being trusted with responsibilities sooner, making choices that had significant effects on the organization.

He thought of his daughter. Like the young professionals he saw rising in the corporate world, she had her own dreams, her own capabilities. And for the first time, Vikram realized that he could let go of the notion that success was about climbing the corporate ladder at a steady pace. It wasn't about waiting for "experience" to come with age. It was about creating space for talent to grow and shine, regardless of the years spent in the workforce.

His thoughts turned inward once again. Vikram had long carried the weight of believing that the next achievement was always just around the corner. But now, he knew that the real change came not from chasing that next rung on the ladder but from letting go of the obsession with the climb altogether.

As he gazed at the horizon, he saw it all clearly—the road ahead, the path that would lead him to a more balanced life, where work and personal fulfilment coexisted, where family and ambition could walk hand in hand.

But first, he had to make peace with the truth: *The obsession was never really about success. It was about proving something to himself, about feeling enough.*

And now, Vikram knew, he was ready to let go of that need.

XXIX

A Shift in the Narrative

Vikram sat by the window, looking out at the skyline as the evening sun dipped below the horizon. The world outside seemed to continue in its relentless pace, yet here, in this moment, he found himself quietly reflective. His thoughts had been churning for weeks now, and the lines between what he was supposed to do and what he wanted to do were starting to blur. His journey had never been about the destination, but the constant motion, the chase, and the obsession to rise higher, to do more. And now, as he stood at the crossroads of his professional life, something inside him was changing.

Aarushi, his wife, had always been a grounding force in his life. Through the years of challenges, late-night calls, and endless boardroom battles, she had been his rock. Yet, in recent months, she'd noticed a shift in Vikram. He seemed different. Less driven by the need to conquer and more focused on finding peace.

Over dinner, as they sat together at the table, Aarushi finally broke the silence. "Vikram, you've always told me how important it is to be on the move, to always be striving for more. But I see the toll it's taking on you. On us. Have you ever thought about what would happen if you slowed down for a while? If you stopped chasing the next big thing and just lived in the moment?"

Vikram looked at her, his mind racing. For years, he had been consumed by his work, the pressure to achieve, to be someone. He had been too focused on the external, on proving his worth. But what was it all for? Was this relentless pursuit of success truly making him happy? Was it even sustainable?

He had always believed that success was the ultimate answer, but lately, he wasn't so sure. He thought about his own upbringing—the pressure to succeed, to prove himself—and how that same expectation had shaped his every decision. But what if that wasn't the only way? What if success wasn't just about climbing the corporate ladder or achieving external validation? What if it was about finding a sense of balance, peace, and fulfilment in the process?

"I think you're right, Aarushi," Vikram replied slowly, his voice tinged with uncertainty. "I've been so focused on what's ahead, I haven't really thought about what's right here, right now."

Aarushi smiled softly, her eyes filled with understanding. "It's not about abandoning your ambition, Vikram. It's about rethinking what you're chasing. What if you're already enough?"

Vikram leaned back in his chair, his mind spinning with the possibilities. For years, he had been conditioned to believe that more was always better. But was it? Was there room to redefine success, not just for himself, but for the generations to come?

His thoughts turned to their children. They had grown up watching Vikram's obsession with his work, the late nights and constant stress. But they were different. They were questioning the very definition of success, choosing paths that were more aligned with their own passions and strengths. The world was changing, and with it, so were the expectations of what it meant to be successful.

Perhaps, it was time to let go of the relentless pursuit of more. To allow the next generation to define success on their own terms, without the pressure of following the same path. The obsession with careers, with climbing ladders, could be replaced with a healthier, more holistic approach to life.

"What if we taught them that it's okay to live life on their own terms?" Vikram mused aloud. "What if we gave them the freedom to choose what makes them truly happy, rather than forcing them into predefined moulds?"

Aarushi's smile widened. "That's exactly it. They don't need to follow your path, or mine. They need to create their own."

As Vikram sat there, the weight of the conversation sinking in, he felt a sense of peace he hadn't known in years. Maybe it was time to let go of the obsession that had defined him for so long. Maybe it was time to live life differently—slower, more intentionally, and with a focus on what truly mattered.

It wasn't an easy decision, but it was the right one. For him. For Aarushi. And for the next generation, who deserved the space to explore their own potential without the weight of expectations hanging over them.

XXX

A New Definition of Success

Vikram had always been a man in motion. His life, like a well-oiled machine, had been driven by goals—ambitions that once seemed like the only measure of his worth. But the recent days of reflection, conversations with Aarushi, and moments of quiet contemplation had shifted something deep within him. He felt as though he was standing at the threshold of a new chapter, one where he had the power to redefine what success truly meant.

The idea had been brewing for some time, but now, it was clear as daylight. For so many years, Vikram had been obsessed with the idea of more—more money, more achievements, more recognition. But he began to realize that all these pursuits had only been filling a void that never quite seemed to disappear. The more he had chased these fleeting victories, the further he seemed to drift from what he had actually wanted from life.

And then there were the children. Vikram had always believed in pushing them to be the best, to achieve more, just as he had. But now, seeing the world through a different lens, he understood that perhaps there was another path. One that didn't involve living up to someone else's standards, but instead, one where they were allowed to carve their own identity, explore their passions, and pursue their own sense of fulfilment—on their own terms.

As he sat down at the kitchen table one evening, his thoughts turned inward. Aarushi had been right all along: the obsession to achieve more, to be always in pursuit of the next thing, was not sustainable. It was a fleeting, empty promise that left him feeling hollow, no matter how many goals he reached.

"I've spent so many years building this image of success," Vikram muttered to himself. "But at what cost? What have I truly built?"

The question echoed in his mind as he looked around his home, at the life he had created, and the family he had raised. Success had never been a destination; it had always been a journey. But it wasn't until now that he realized that the journey was about much more than just the destination itself.

Vikram had grown up with the idea that success was quantifiable—that it could be measured by external markers: titles, positions, and material wealth. It was how society had trained him to think, how his family had instilled in him the need to constantly prove himself. But now, he questioned the very foundation of that belief.

The world had changed. The next generation—the younger leaders, the innovators—had begun to redefine success in their own way. They were not shackled by the same old notions of what was important. They were willing to embrace uncertainty, take risks, and explore what it meant to live a life of purpose. They were not as afraid to fail, and they certainly weren't obsessed with accumulating accolades and titles.

Vikram felt a deep sense of admiration for this shift in thinking, especially as he watched his children navigate their own paths. Their approach to life was different from his, yet there was something invigorating about their ability to chase their passions without being burdened by the weight of conventional expectations.

He thought of his own journey—the years of stress, the missed moments, the relentless push for more. But in that reflection, he also saw the person he had become. The change wasn't just external—it was internal too. The decision to let go of the obsession to prove himself, to stop measuring his worth by the number of achievements he had accumulated, was freeing. He was finally beginning to embrace the idea that life wasn't about being better than everyone else—it was about being true to himself.

This realization was, in many ways, liberating. It meant that he could start living for the present, instead of always chasing after the future. He could embrace the imperfection of life, the quiet moments, and the simple joys without feeling the pressure to constantly perform.

But it wasn't just about him. Vikram knew that this shift in mindset could influence the way he raised his children. They didn't need to follow his exact footsteps or his path.

They didn't need to carry the same weight of expectations that had once weighed him down. What mattered was that they found their own way—one that resonated with their true passions and interests.

As Vikram sat there, deep in thought, Aarushi joined him at the table. She could see the change in his expression, the calm that had settled over him, the burden that had lifted.

"Are you alright?" she asked softly, her voice filled with concern yet tinged with hope.

Vikram smiled, his eyes meeting hers. "I'm more than alright," he said, his voice steady. "I'm finally beginning to understand that success doesn't look the same for everyone. It's not just about doing more or achieving more. It's about finding peace in what we do, and the people we share it with."

Aarushi's smile was a reflection of the relief they both felt in that moment.

"It's never been about the titles, Vikram. It's about living a life that feels right for you."

And so, in that moment, the new definition of success was born—not in titles or accolades, but in the freedom to be authentic, to embrace life as it came, and to let go of the obsession that had defined Vikram's journey for so long.

As he looked out the window, watching the world go by, he realized that his journey had just begun.

It was no longer about chasing more. It was about savouring the moments, embracing the imperfect beauty of life, and guiding his children to do the same.

The future, for the first time, felt full of possibilities—not to prove, but to live.

XXXI
The Weight of Expectations

Vikram sat in the living room of his apartment, the silence around him almost deafening. Aarushi had gone to bed early, leaving him alone with his thoughts. It was during these moments of stillness that his mind wandered back to the pivotal moments of his life—the moments that had shaped him into the person he was now. He had been so caught up in chasing success, climbing one rung after another on the ladder of ambition, that he had neglected to question why he was doing it in the first place.

His thoughts drifted back to the last time he had visited his parents in their home, a few years ago. It had been one of those rare occasions where he could feel the weight of his own identity—who he was, who they wanted him to be. Sitting in the living room, sipping on masala chai, his parents had casually dropped the subject that had lingered in the air for years.

"Beta, when will you settle down? When will you give us some good news? You've always been so busy with your work and success. We want to see you happy, truly happy."

The question was gentle, almost loving. But beneath it lay a pressure, one that had been building for years. It wasn't just about career anymore. It was about Vikram's identity, his purpose, his path in life. He could see it in their eyes—the unspoken desire for him to conform to what they thought was the "right" way of living. To have the perfect job, the ideal family, the life that would bring them the pride they believed he deserved.

But it wasn't just about his parents. It was the collective voice of society, echoing in his ears—the voice that told him that success could only be measured by what you had achieved, by how many hours you worked, how much you earned. This relentless voice had led him to an unspoken belief that if he didn't keep pushing forward, he would be seen as a failure.

Vikram shifted in his chair, feeling the weight of those memories, those words from the past. He had lived for so long under the illusion that his worth was tied to his career, to the numbers, the promotions, and the material gains. But now, with the distance of time and a growing sense of clarity, he began to realize that he had been chasing someone else's version of success.

The Turning Point

As he sat there, staring at the stillness of his reflection in the window, the quiet realization settled in: he didn't want to live for someone else's expectations anymore. His pursuit of success had been motivated by the need for validation, to prove that he was worthy of the titles, the achievements, and the accolades. But now, Vikram felt a need to redefine what success meant for him—not as a comparison to others, not as a chase to fill a societal void, but as a reflection of what made him truly happy.

He thought about Aarushi, their daughter, and the new perspective he was developing about life. He wanted to give her the freedom to define her own version of success, not to be shackled by the expectations that had shaped his own life. He wanted her to understand that real fulfilment came from living authentically, from doing what aligned with her values, not from meeting someone else's standards.

Vikram closed his eyes, allowing the quiet to envelop him, as he let go of the past—a past shaped by external validation. The journey ahead was one of self-discovery, not in the chase for recognition, but in the pursuit of personal peace and fulfilment. The obsession, he realized, could be left behind.

XXXII

The Quiet Wisdom

Vikram sat quietly in the dimly lit room, his eyes focused on the note in front of him. It was a simple sheet of paper, folded neatly and adorned with his wife's elegant handwriting. Aarushi had always been a woman of few words, yet each word she wrote carried weight, a quiet wisdom that always seemed to penetrate straight to his heart.

The note began with a gentle tone, as though she was speaking to him in person.

"Vikram, I know you're struggling. I can see it in the way you carry yourself, the way your mind races even when your body is still. You are constantly fighting against expectations—yours, mine, and the world's. But you need to understand, success isn't a race. You've always believed that to matter, you must keep going, keep achieving, keep chasing the next thing. But I need you to know something important: you already matter. Just as you are, right now."

Vikram's heart tightened. She had a way of cutting through his defences. Aarushi knew him better than anyone, even the parts of himself he refused to acknowledge.

"Remember when we first met? When we talked about our dreams, our desires, and how we wanted to live a life that was free from the pressures of the world? Somewhere along the way, you let the weight of expectations steal that from you. And while I understand your need to fulfil your obligations, please remember that the greatest gift you can give to yourself—and to me—is peace. I don't need you to be perfect, Vikram. I just need you to be present."

The words hit him harder than he anticipated. It wasn't just about his work, his career, or the societal pressures. It was about him. His internal conflict, the constant pull between ambition and the quieter, simpler life he had once longed for.

Aarushi's note continued: "I want you to start looking at life through a different lens. Our daughter sees the world with a sense of freedom, and I want you to see it that way too. Let go of the idea that you have to climb every mountain, cross every obstacle, and be someone else's definition of success. Let's find peace together. Not in the rush to succeed, but in the quiet moments we create."

The weight of those words lingered in the room long after he finished reading. Aarushi's wisdom was never loud, never demanding. But her presence, even in these silent notes, was enough to shake him to his core.

Vikram folded the note carefully and tucked it into his pocket. He knew what he had to do. It wasn't about making a grand gesture or changing everything overnight. It was about finding balance, about choosing to live with intention rather than in the frenzy of constant pursuit.

And as he sat there, a calmness began to settle over him. He knew that this wasn't the end of his journey.

It was just another turning point—one that would lead him back to the life he once dreamed of, the life where success was measured not by what he could achieve, but by the peace he could find within himself.

XXXIII

Breaking the Cycle

Vikram's mind raced as the plane descended, the familiar hum of the engines mixing with his thoughts. It was a surreal feeling, this coming home after months of running, building, chasing, and convincing himself that success could only be found in the relentless pursuit of more. The plane's wheels touched the ground, signalling his return to a life that, in its simplicity, had long been waiting for him to reawaken to its truth.

He had spent years defining himself through titles, accolades, and achievements—each step further away from the man he was and closer to the man society expected him to become. But now, as he looked at the city through the plane window, he wondered if all the recognition he had chased was worth the cost.

Vikram felt a stirring in his chest—an unfamiliar sensation that had been quietly growing inside him for the past few weeks. It was a desire for something different, something more meaningful than titles. It was the pull of rediscovery, of remembering who he was before the obsession of success clouded his vision.

And then there was Aarushi.

Her note, simple yet profound, had struck a chord deep within him. He could still feel the words on the paper: *"Find the rhythm of life, Vikram. Not the beat of the rat race, but the melody that resonates with your soul."* Her wisdom, so grounded and yet so transformative, was a message he had long neglected to hear.

But it was clear now. He had spent so much of his life chasing a version of success that had never really belonged to him. It was a success built on the foundation of societal expectations, the pressure to be more, do more, and achieve more than anyone around him. But the reality was, it had left him weary and disconnected from everything that truly mattered.

As he made his way home, the streets that had once felt like a blur of deadlines, meetings, and fleeting moments of success now seemed more like a path to healing. He began to see things differently—the people, the moments, the choices. This was not the same city that had once driven him to push harder, faster, and further.

This was a city that had been waiting for him to come back, not as a career-driven, success-obsessed man, but as a human being who had forgotten the value of being present.

Vikram knew that breaking the cycle wouldn't be easy. He had spent decades reinforcing the idea that life was about climbing higher, faster, and achieving more. But now, it seemed that the only thing left for him to achieve was peace. Peace with himself, peace with his past, and peace with the people who had always loved him without conditions.

The hardest part of this realization was acknowledging that the cycle he had been living in wasn't just about him—it was about everyone around him. It was about the pressure society placed on individuals, especially men, to prove their worth through professional success, titles, and external validation. The same cycle that had consumed him was the one that had likely consumed so many others.

The thought was unsettling. For so long, Vikram had convinced himself that his path was his alone. But the truth was, it wasn't. It was part of a larger societal pattern—one that affected so many others.

As he entered his home, Aarushi greeted him with a warm smile, her eyes filled with the same understanding she had always shown him. She didn't ask about his meetings, his travels, or his latest achievements. Instead, she simply asked, "How are you feeling?"

For the first time in a long time, Vikram realized that the question wasn't about success. It wasn't about the race. It wasn't about the future. It was about now.

And in that moment, he finally understood.

He wasn't meant to be a part of the cycle anymore.

He was meant to break it, to find a new path forward, one that allowed him to live a life that wasn't defined by obsession but by meaning.

He hugged Aarushi tightly. No words were necessary. She knew.

Vikram had finally found his way home.

From The Desk Of Author

Dear Reader,

As you've travelled alongside Vikram's journey through the pages of this book, I hope you've come to understand that "living in the suitcase" is more than just a literal experience. It's a metaphor, one that encapsulates the struggle between professional obsession and personal fulfilment.

At first glance, a suitcase may seem like an ordinary object—used for travel, for moving between places, for carrying what we think we need. But as we dig deeper into Vikram's world, we see that the suitcase becomes a symbol of a life in motion, constantly shifting and adapting to external demands, with little room for pause or reflection. Vikram's story is not just about the physicality of travel—boarding flights, moving between hotels, living out of a suitcase—but about the emotional and mental toll it takes.

To live in a suitcase is to live on the edge of constant motion, to be caught in the whirlwind of societal expectations, career ambitions, and the unrelenting pressures that come with them. It's a life where you move forward, but never fully arrive.

Vikram's journey reflects the internal conflict that so many of us experience in today's world: the relentless pursuit of success, the societal belief that we must sacrifice everything else for our careers, and the toll it takes on our personal lives and relationships. For Vikram, the suitcase is not just a container of belongings—it is a container of dreams, of unspoken sacrifices, of missed moments, and of emotional baggage that he carries with him everywhere.

But here's the paradox—the suitcase is also a tool of hope. It symbolizes the journey towards something greater, the aspiration to create a better life for ourselves and our loved ones. However, without reflection, it becomes a cage.

Through Vikram's story, I've tried to highlight that the obsession with "living out of the suitcase"—the never-ending travel, the constant professional demands, the societal pressure to "achieve more" at the cost of personal well-being—is not a sustainable way of living. The toll it takes on one's health, relationships, and sense of self can be immense. But more importantly, it obscures the true purpose of life, which is not just about success or recognition, but about living fully, deeply, and authentically.

This book is an invitation to all those who find themselves caught in the cycle of professional obsession. To those who are constantly on the move, physically or emotionally, in pursuit of a life that feels just out of reach. It's an invitation to stop, unpack the suitcase, and reconsider what truly matters.

The real message I hope you take away from this book is that you don't need to "live in the suitcase" forever. You can choose to step outside the cycle, embrace a life of balance, and break free from the pressures that keep you trapped in constant motion. It's not easy, and it doesn't happen overnight, but it begins with a decision—to pause, to reflect, and to live with intention.

In closing, I'd like to thank you for walking this journey with Vikram. Whether you saw parts of yourself in his story or found new insights through his experiences, I hope it has sparked something within you—a desire to live a life that is not just about reaching the next destination, but about truly embracing the journey itself.

May you unpack your suitcase, step into your true potential, and live the life you've always dreamed of.

With gratitude and reflection,

Deepak Sharma